THE LIVING LORE

THE SHADES OF THE ABYSS

THE LIVING LORE
THE SHADES OF THE ABYSS

F. LOCKHAVEN

E.J. ILLAR

Editors

David Aretha

Andrea VanRyken

André MacLean

Grace Lockhaven

TWISTED KEY
publishing

2021

CONTENTS

I

A young man awoke in his bed after a startling and impressive dream. As soon as he was up, before he even opened his eyes, rose from his position, or even let out a sigh from the comfort of his pillow, he leaned far to the side and reached for a quill pen on his nightstand to write with. A piece of paper was already prepared, and he blindly scribbled the details down.

In those brief moments between dreaming and waking, Baxter Movish opened his eyes in a tight squint to greet the first morning light that crept in from the narrow slats of his window. The wooden blinds were drawn as tight as they could but still let in the light he so resented every morning—just enough that he couldn't sleep past the first bells in the city.

Once he finally opened his eyes and brushed the curls away from his face, he looked down and saw his writing hand had lazed onto the table, half-numb and reeling with the pain of pins and needles. He shook it off and sat up properly on his bed. Another night had passed, which meant another day had started, and the plans for that day were what put him onto his feet.

He redressed himself clumsily into his scholarly apparel. A classic, tie-down petticoat over his regular, airy, wide-sleeve blouse, which he buttoned with detached collars over his wrists to keep the fabric out of the way of his working hands. His trousers reached down to his knees and tied into his socks, which rose from his feet. His shoes were buckled into place, except for the right one. It was just old enough that it was starting to wear out over his arch.

"Well, that's wonderful," he sighed. He took the chance of speaking to clear his throat and get his voice reoriented into its ideal tone, deepened with his early, burgeoning maturity. If he cleared it enough times, he thought it wouldn't crack so much during the day into his younger, higher tones. With his garments assembled, he threw on his hooded robe and clasped it under his neck collar. It was still a junior's robe in size and standing, with a single line of gold trim at the bottom of the dark blue, hip-length fabric and another golden ring around the hood line.

He stood in front of a full-height mirror that stood a bit taller than he did and admired his appearance. "Perhaps today," he wondered aloud, "Master Lothan will stop being coy and recommend me properly." He gave it a moment of thought, put his Master in his mind, then sighed with a defeated expression. "Or he'll tell me to wait until next year again."

Baxter was prepared to move out immediately. He readied his mind and his heart for another day at the Archive, but before he left, he remembered the passive writing he'd done while half-asleep. His dream notes were on his nightstand, and he didn't want to wait until the evening to read them. What he wrote down was still half a mystery even to him, so he picked it up and prepared to gawk at his own terrible, illegible scrawls.

"Dreamed of Abyss," he read out loud. "Mountain and Sea. Shades, shadows: no bodies or light. Reference: The Old World Comp. Volume VI, Volume VIII, Volume E: Daemondimonium, Light and Dark Shadows."

Baxter was an apprentice cryptographist, a reader of concealed words in ancient texts made of languages from the ages of antiquity that had lapsed into legend. He'd read impossible stories told by real people in dictation that were reprinted by hand and kept in the Archive for restoration and recontextualizing as both a duty and privilege of his position, all because he loved to read. He'd learned of all the world's most arcane legends and myths, and yet his own writing was the most confusing thing he'd ever read.

"I suppose I'll…give those a look-over," he sighed. He put the paper down like he was disappointed in it for being incomprehensible, but at least he recognized a few things about it. It reminded him of the titles of books he still had to organize. All the more reason he had to leave for the day.

He left his room and ambled down the stairs, ignoring the smell of cooked, greasy meat that wafted through the air. Meat was a slumber-inducing food, and he needed his mind to be racing as early as possible. However, his brothers and father felt a different way.

"Oi, Baxy!" a voice called out. He turned at the foot of the stairs and saw the dining room full-up with happy eaters, including some guests—friends of his brothers who came by before work. "Leaving already?" The caller was his oldest brother, the head worker of the city's renovations crew, Bart. Bart had eaten so much ham he appeared half-pig in the haze of the early morning. He sweated easily and had a pudgy nose to match his pudgy arms, back and waist. He held up a fork with a slab of wet ham and wiggled it around, causing the drippings to flicker out onto the floor for the cats to lick up. "We got food for you too."

"If he begs, maybe," another voice called out, gravely and ornery-sounding. It came from his slovenly, bloated brother Barny who wielded a loaf of bread in one hand and thick slabs of bacon in the other, fork not required. Just seeing meat, cooked or raw, in his brother's greasy hands made Baxter visibly grimace, which his brothers were fast to notice.

"Oh, go on, then!" Bart called out. "Eat your books, you love them so much. Get some roughage in you!"

The table then started chanting "Roughage! Roughage!" over and over until Baxter was out of the house. He sighed and took a pause at the door to calm his mind. His family, the only family that he had in the world, seemed to only exist to mock him for his own given talents and his steady-learned skills. He was the only one in the house who could read, including his mother and father. Each morning he left with that solitude on his shoulder, like a weight he couldn't shake. A burden of responsibility that mocked him in his own home.

His home was located in the Festival Quarter, as it was called. It was the kindest way the city planners could think to phrase the slums near the base of the city where the day workers, laborers, and uneducated families all lived. The richer, more advantaged classes all lived up the hill toward the old Royal Quarter, which had once been home to the nobles. Even without the presence of a king, a monarchy, or any kind of single ruling party, the old ways persisted, as they always did.

Checcheri was a grand city, a Corner State in the Vincian Empire. One of the seven Great Cities of the High World. It was a place where trade began and ended, not a port town or a travel-through place like others were. Merchants lived in Checcheri. Their headquarters were in the Trade Quarter, esteemed and regal palaces that rivaled the old noble houses further up the hill. As such, the city prospered as many others did, all affected by the great Age of Enlightenment that spread across the lands.

It was a time where the wars of old had long since ended, and the wounds they had opened were healed over but not forgotten. The legacies that the ancestors and noble families brought from the Old World were rooted in and gave birth to the flowering trees of industry over time. The city was built on the wealth of that knowledge—the knowledge espoused in the many legends and in the songs and plays performed to commemorate that historic past. Knowledge was the most important currency, even rivaling gold. So, despite his lower-class upbringing, Baxter consistently felt like he was the richest of the rich because he knew what few others could ever learn.

After reflecting on his surroundings, he looked up and began marching up the street until he left the humble trappings of his lowborn home and made his way into the Arts District. It was an age of art, an era of creation and creativity the likes of which had never been recorded in history. The peace brought more than monetary prominence to Vincia; it also brought purpose to its people's idle hands, allowing them to give their talent and skills to a higher plane of existence than what they physically could see. It was an era ruled by the mind and not the body. Although, from Baxter's perspective, things were still very much swayed by the bodies of others—at least in the Festival Quarter.

"Baxter!" someone called out. Baxter turned and saw someone heading his way, a tall and strong-looking man whose height and observable layers of muscles betrayed the fact that he was Baxter's age and no older. Derek Solly, his childhood friend, ran up with a chunk of marble stone hoisted up onto his shoulder that weighed at least a hundred pounds if not more, and he treated it like it was a basket of laundry.

"Careful, Derek," Baxter warned, shying away from his friend's dangerous workload. "You could crush a man flat with that."

Derek looked over and rubbed his cheek against the stone. "Oh, this?" he asked. "No, no, it's fine here. It's not going anywhere. And I'm safe already, see?" He tried to angle himself down and pointed at the space between the rock and his shoulder. Baxter saw a padded blanket serving as the brace that kept his arm from breaking against the weight but questioned its effectiveness on keeping Derek's face safe. "It can't go sliding around like this, yeah?"

"Good thinking," Baxter approved. "What's it for, though?"

"So, there's a guy," Derek began, "trying to carve a woman's bust. I mean like, the bust of her bust, but from up her—"

"I get it," Baxter interrupted.

"He's the son of a Merchant but wants to be a Sculptor and stuff, and he keeps messing up, and the woman he's sculpting keeps getting pissy and yelling that his work's all wrong. And he snapped back once at her, saying it's his art, and his interpretation is closer to truth than what he sees or something—so she socks him right in the nose, tells him to start over for the ninth time already! He's buying up marble from the quarry wholesale, skipping the markets, and we're getting full price."

"Noblemen are certainly generous," Baxter said sarcastically.

"Kinda skittish, though," Derek added, countering Baxter's backhanded compliment.

"Well, he may not pay you if it breaks," Baxter warned again.

"Yeah, I got it," Derek said, hoisting it up to make it look somehow safer in his already controlled arms. "Aye, find a heavy book today and pick it up over your head. You'll feel better."

"I'll try that," Baxter called out. He kept on his way, feeling his chest grow a little lighter. Derek was his oldest friend and the only man without literacy that Baxter felt he could get close to. Derek didn't care for the arts or culture or anything that he seemed to most commonly work on, but he was strong, in body and heart. Friendly to anybody, regardless of their class or standing, Derek never looked down on anyone nor spoke out against those who looked down on him.

On his final approach to the Archive, a building he could see for blocks around that oriented him around the city every day, Baxter neglected to look directly ahead and ran into someone. The impact caused him to stumble backward, and his shoe buckle popped open, causing him to fall right out of it and slip onto his back. He sighed when he landed—the frustration was greater than his pain—and he sat up to see who he had offended with his negligence.

Curiously, the one who stood before him was a girl. She wore a well-kept green dress with an apron that had the symbol of the Porter Guild on it, a covered wagon circled by a coil of ivy. She looked upset but unshaken, and judging by the force of their collision, also as sturdy as the marble chunk that Derek was carrying.

"Do excuse yourself," she said. "I can't wait forever."

"Oh, sorry," Baxter replied. He stayed sitting and reached over for his shoe. His trousers were dusty, he realized. He struggled to latch the buckle again, as it had clearly broken the whole way through, and his pause caused the girl to give a very impatient, tired sigh.

"If you can't apologize properly, then pay better attention," she demanded.

"Of course I will," he said. "Of course."

She huffed and stormed away. Baxter finally got up after forcing the buckle shut at the expense of his freedom. His shoe was essentially locked in place with no way to free it but cutting the leather. He looked on as the girl left and carved a path ahead of her out of the busy but hastily retreating travelers who didn't want to stand in her way. If only he'd looked ahead, he would have done the same.

The Merchant Guilds and their workers had the right of way on every road, even through the Royal Quarter. The Porter Guild was responsible for deliveries throughout the city. They brought goods to important businesses or private estates that came from all over the country and even transported imports from the Old World. They were contracted by very high-paying and esteemed people, so the contents of what they carried were highly valued. In another town or another part of Checcheri, a girl like her would be the target of some maligned and criminal mind who valued her goods far more than her own well-being. Baxter considered such a crook unfortunate to go against her, though. She carried herself with more assertion than Derek did.

At last, with no further distractions, Baxter reached Main Street, a road that stretched all the way from the gatehouse of the old, historic lower town that used to be the whole of the city to the great castle above, which hosted the new enlightened rulers of the countryside in their mountainous corner of Vincia. Cathedral Row, the lane lined with castle-like churches, was the main thoroughfare of all trade and foot traffic. It was the central road that connected all of the city together and ran uphill in winding grades for horse and cart and offered mounting stairs for the fleet of foot.

Baxter cut across the street, went up one terrace of the hill by the steps, and walked straight up to the Archive. It was one of the largest cathedrals, owning the tallest tower of any building in the city. It was once owned by the priesthood who attempted to use their position as the highest place in all of Checcheri to connect the living world with the realm of divinity, like a great mountain that rose out of the oceans to touch the sacred sky, and extract the power of light for themselves. That was what the legends and the diaries of the builders said at least.

After the Age of Conquest ended and the last wars finished off, the site was abandoned by its former sponsors and was returned to the control of the ruling Emperor of Checcheri, who at the time was a wise man who valued knowledge of the world over the potential of the divine. And so it was that the largest cathedral of its time would become the Archive of all written works, old and new. A library of all human history, from myths to more recent musings of philosophy from the Great Thinkers of the City of Minds, was stored inside.

Baxter took a breath and readied himself to enter again. There were no jockish brutes, dangerous lifting, or intimidating Merchants inside the halls of the Archive. There were only books. All he had to do was learn.

2

There were no walls visible in the Archive, only shelves stacked to the four-story ceiling with books, scrolls, and assemblies of papers that had been collected and collated into bindings over centuries of arduous reclamation work. Factions across the High World and collaborators in the Old World had all gathered together over the Age of Conquest to hoard the texts of fallen civilizations, lost tribes, and the contemporary works of the poets and artists that sprang forth to commemorate the lauded pasts. The result was a massive storage of knowledge—the most in all the world.

For people with time to spare, it was a blessing to have all the information at hand they could ever desire, to learn about the world that passed them by in their daily lives. For those who worked there, it was a burden, since not all the information was so willingly given. The nature of restrictions that layered every single book within the Archive was not based on any rites or cultural passage. Anyone who could read was welcome to peruse through the many halls of tomes, provided that the tomes were still physically readable, and far too many were not. Age had stricken the collection, and many of the great works of the past approached dilapidation and disrepair. The best among them were given new covers and spines by the Binders, but the worst had to be restored letter by letter into new manuscripts by the Scribes.

That was Baxter's job. He didn't just read; he rewrote. It was his duty to read the books that couldn't be opened without losing pages and copy the contents down into newer compendiums, one painful page at a time. Baxter's pain was constant, dulling, and monotonous. The mental strain rivaled the physical as each day blended into the last, and all the information swirled together in a mesh within his mind. It was no surprise that his dreams were incomprehensible when written out since the work of his day required his thoughts to be the same way. But he persevered, never faltering, always steadfast, and never speaking but to practice the pronunciations of the passages he found most interesting. He, along with all the other Scribes and Binders and Painters, loved learning.

Baxter went straight to work as soon as he entered. Each Scribe had a little office off in the side rooms, once used for communal eating, bathing, or the various activities the priesthood of the cathedral had to tend to in order to maintain their massive building project. The tower that the cathedral hosted, which later came to be worshipped in its own right, was the central pillar around which most of the books were stacked. It had become a rounded library shelf, and walkways were built to trace along the architecture like a wooden spider web that surrounded it on many levels. Anyone afraid of heights was forbidden from working there. If they were, they would never be able to retrieve the books stored at the highest point of the Archive to work on them.

Baxter's station consisted of a simple, stout, and wooden desk. He was just tall enough that he didn't have to hunch to do his work unless the book itself was large or taller than it was wide. At his side was a quill pen, and aside that was a well of ink drilled directly into the wooden frame of the desk and covered with a thin sheet of window glass. The black bar on the side measured his progress through the day as well as his storage of ink to write with. When it lost its shimmer, he knew it was running low, which happened no less than three times a day. If he were working on something that intrigued him or something of great importance put onto him by his Master, one of the attendants would refill it for him while he worked.

The books he was working on were all chronicles from the Old World, legends of wars between tribes near the Deep Sea, a region he'd learned about previously from old trade documents, diaries of soldiers during the wars in the Age of Conquest, fisherman parables, creation myths, Abyssal lore, and other such readings. Despite never having seen them, he had read about the Old World countries outside of the Vincian Empire so many times from so many sources he felt like he'd already explored them to death. The only thing he hadn't seen but wanted to were the fantastical legends of magic. But stories were stories, and the written word was never entirely true. Even the biography of a man could tell as many lies as the tall tale spun by that man's own neighbor.

In the course of his day, Baxter would copy down thousands upon thousands of words by hand. From a labor point of view, what he did was just as strenuous and taxing on his body as the heavy-lifting Derek did, just in different ways. His writing arm was lean and taut all the way up to his wrist. Even in the spring of his youth, before he'd even turned twenty and been considered a full-fledged adult by society, he'd battled with the pains and the creaking joints of a far more aged man. Most of the men working in the Archive suffered similar issues. Baxter's talent for learning propelled him into the position at a very young age. He had been working for nearly a year at that point, so the luster of his presence had worn off on the rest of the Archive staff.

"Oh, Baxter," a lady said as she passed by. One of the Custodians responsible for carrying books from their shelves to the tables and replacing older copies with the newly restored revisions tapped the corner of his desk. "Master Lothan asked for you to come by during your first break. He wants to speak with you."

"All right," Baxter said. When he looked up and listened to her, he was suddenly immersed in the sounds of scrawling pens upon pages trailing ink around in infinitely complex shapes and characters, like thousands of cats screeching at a mighty stone wall. "I'll try to keep track of that."

"Okay," she said. She went off to her duties while Baxter began his. He looked to the side, to a row of hourglasses held in rotating wheels with labels beneath them. Each measured a different amount of time and had different purposes. The largest one determined breaks, which happened every four hours, and each worker was afforded two throughout the day. Most Scribes stayed eight hours at most, yet a few stretched their time out to ten out of love for the work and to be in the good graces of their superiors. Baxter was a special case, however, and planned to stay for twelve hours each day. He was the Apprentice Master Archivist, directly working under Master Lothan the Learned.

Once his first break came around, signaled by the chime of a bell that the hourglass made once all of its weight hit its bottom half, Baxter stood up and assessed the work he had completed. His pace was average, but his work was always flawless, and he made one extra step of effort as he wrote from page to page. He read the work itself. He didn't just write the words as he saw them, but he understood them as well, and on rare occasions in which the authors of ancient history were mistaken or too hasty in their own recollections, he corrected their grammar and spelling too. Only for the most common words, though. Names and places or strange ideas stayed as they were.

He had read in the vast journal he had just replicated about a man's travel to a craggy range of mountains. There was the fabled country of Hassah in the Old World, home to the source of all the world's evils and the birthplace of Shades, the apparitions responsible for all of mankind's plagues and unseen hardships. All malaise, anxiety, anger, and hatred born into men's hearts unprompted was born from Shades, or so the man had reckoned, and so he sought the place of their birth: the Mouth of the Abyss.

It wasn't particularly exciting, but the mention of the Abyss gave Baxter a slight chill. It reminded him of his mid-waking scribbles, the mad unconscious ramblings of his mind put onto paper as a reminder for him to try and read more about it. One way or another, his dreaming self was being fulfilled. He kept it in mind as he hiked the long walk from the scribe alley, past the halls of shelves and into the sacred tower, which served as the keep for all the most important and valuable books in the Archive, tended to only by the most trusted staff as selected by the Master Archivist himself.

The inside of the tower, which was once a place of worship, became just another corner for dry storage of the historic materials. Books were only piled up if they could endure the weight and contact of other books. Most were spread out and kept totally separate. Some were even kept in chests that took up space on every floor of the steep, high tower. The stairs spiraled upward, and every seven feet a new floor was built and was likewise covered with books. Places of worship—once meant to feel closer to an ancient God—were just convenient spaces where moisture wasn't a problem. It was so temperate that mold eventually stopped growing outright on any books afflicted and would in time die and become flakes of dust upon the pages.

The Master Archivist was always somewhere near the top or at the very top itself. The tower was twice as tall as the cathedral, reaching nearly a hundred feet off the ground. It was like walking all the way uphill to get to the Archive itself all over again. Baxter endured the steps and stopped his mind from wandering into discontent with thoughts of the books he'd read or still had to read. His mind was tied up with questions about the Abyss and its nature in mythology. He wondered if such a place were real in the vast expanse of the explored world. An ocean without light beneath the ground and a mountain that connected its lifeless denizens to the world above. Literally, it seemed impossible, but it had to have some greater meaning, at least enough to invade his dreams.

If anyone knew the deeper meanings of ancient lore, it would be Master Lothan. Baxter finally reached the floor where his Master dwelled and saw the man pick up a book with a firm, steady grip on its pages. He turned, and his beard turned with him, gray around the mouth and black just inches away from his face. His age ate away at the color of his hair from the roots, but his solid, youthful face persisted, with only wrinkles present where he smiled.

"There you are," he said. "I was worried you might have forgotten again."

"Not today," Baxter replied as he caught his breath. "Master, what do you need of me?"

"Today," Lothan spoke with some importance, "is the day you expand your repertoire of skills for the Archive. Starting tomorrow, you will begin work in an apprenticeship as a Binder."

"A Binder?" Baxter repeated in disbelief.

"And we shall start with this book," Lothan said. He held the mighty tome outward, and in his presentation, his grip loosened just enough that a page from the middle slipped out. Then another, then several more, and then the entire book's contents, aside from the few pages still held on near the beginning and end, spilled out onto the floor like an overturned bucket of water. Baxter watched it happen, all emotion gone from his face, and he turned to leave.

"That was an accident!" Lothan exclaimed. He put the shell of the book on the table at his side and bent over to pick the pages up. "Hurry, Baxter, get the pages before they—Agh!"

"Master?" Baxter saw Lothan fall onto his side with his arms stuck in place.

"My back," Lothan groaned. "I think I pulled it."

"Picking up paper?" Baxter asked.

"Go down and get Farcellus," Lothan bade, wagging his arms from his crumpled position on the floor. "He's…he's a masseuse. He can fix this."

Baxter took a few steps down, just enough that he could lean his arms on the floor of the room and peer through the slats of the banister that shielded the stairs from sudden falls. "Can't you just lie flat and stretch?"

"Come on, boy," Lothan argued. "It's just a quick up and down again. This is important!"

"What if I pull my legs and fall all the way down the tower from here?" Baxter asked nonchalantly.

Lothan looked through strained eyes at the boy who had become nonplussed by his anguish; so, he stopped. He straightened up his back, stopped pretending, and stood back up.

"You're getting too smart," Lothan said, taking a lecturing tone suddenly. "Seeing through my blunders is one thing, but if you end up strictly analyzing every facet of life, you'll become disappointed with it in no time. Now, uh…." He looked down at the floor and pointed around. His voice became much quieter but still authoritative. "Help me…please."

"Yes, Master," Baxter said. They picked the pages up, reordered them, and for the rest of that day Baxter worked under Lothan the Learned on the careful and precarious art of binding books together again. He lamented the loss of his preferred duty of Scribe work, but it was all part of the necessary steps he had to take. It was his ambition to become an Archivist like his mentor, and it was his mentor's desire to see that ambition through. Together, they worked awfully long to repair the damaged book, and by the time they were done, it was evening, and the rest of the day workers at the Archive had been dismissed home.

Baxter left as well, and only after setting foot outside in the setting sun did he realize with anguish that he had forgotten to ask Lothan all of his questions. "That darned paper gag!" he hissed under his breath. He pulled up his hood over his head and tucked the rim over his eyes. His Master's charismatic jovial attitude had once again disrupted what Baxter thought was the more important act of learning. It wasn't unusual but was always frustrating. At least, in Baxter's mind, when he became the Master Archivist, such things would never have to happen again.

At least the day had not concluded without some further adventure in learning. As he and Lothan had pieced the book back together, he managed to glean some knowledge from it. Particularly about the founding of Vincia. The book turned out to be a tome of the old wars, a collection of reports from battles arranged chronologically, which served his and his

Master's purposes well in reordering the fallen pages. The book told of the eventual rise of the Guild House of the Vinci family, which went on to become the military and economic power that led a collection of allied city-states to victory against the standing armies of foreign foes.

Every day he learned something new, and so every day he drew closer to his goal just by doing what was expected of him. Never any adventures or hard trials of battle, but by reading through them after the fact, he managed to piece together the meaning behind them. It made him not want for travel or expeditions into the unknown because all that knowledge was already collected before him in the form of books. All he had to do was read, and his life felt well-lived….

3

A young woman with hair tied up in a short bun behind her head and an apron marked with the Porter's Guild crest walked down the street with a basket swinging in her hand. Eidel Laun walked home from her busy day of bussing packages up and down the great Checcheri streets from one Quarter of the city to another. She had a stern face, holding back a great scowl from her pursed lips.

Her final compensation at her long day's end was a paltry dinner. Inside the basket was a baked quail breast with stale bread rolls and a shallow cup of fried cabbage and carrots that was left over from the guildhall kitchen, all wrapped up together in a cheesecloth covering to keep it warm.

It was all she could get with her pocket money. The Porter's Guild was important, but that didn't make them rich. Most of their money went to various insurance agencies they had to appease just to keep the prominence of their business within the city walls. Without such certifications, noble families and other

Merchant houses wouldn't allow them to handle their important, exotic goods. To stay in business, they had to bleed out all the money they had every day while the rest of the city, laborers and scholars alike, took home the full share of their working wages for themselves.

The dilemma that plagued Eidel's family had embittered her greatly. She spent each night walking home with spite visible on her brow, such that no one dared approach her, not even with cruel intentions. There was no doubt in the harshest criminal's mind that she would make the loudest, messiest scene despite her standing—and nothing was worse for a passing criminal than a junction made by the Guild's private justice system.

The Porter's house she belonged to was near the old town at the base of the city. It was just in sight of the historic ward's ancient walls, the last and latest line of defense ever arisen since the Age of Conquest so long ago. They blocked the sun as it rose, which caused her to wake every morning in the dark to start her day. Just another inconvenience that stirred up malcontent in her heart. By the end of it all, when her waking hours expired and exhaustion took its hold, she knew she would be too tired to even feel her hatred, and that lapse into an emotionless tiredness was what she valued most. Not hating the world was what she considered close to being asleep.

She wandered inside the single-floor home connected to the two-story carriage garage and looked around. Some candles were lit, but it appeared that no one was home. The interior was wide-open. Walls to the garage and bedrooms on the opposite side were the only things blocking her vision. It was a home fitting for one of the lower families, the unfortunate ones who were paid to walk instead of paid to send others out on the porting. A lower family, even in the upper-class of Merchants, was no different than a laborer's family, and as Porters, they couldn't even read their own contracts to renegotiate.

It didn't bother her at all to be home alone. It gave her enough time to come down from the inconveniences of her day in a safe way without needing to listen to her father's constant, beaten-down lectures. All he talked about was the old-family pride, the way of the Guilds, the duty they had to uphold, the honor in service. It was all defeated talk from a man she thought couldn't sink any lower down the social ladder. She was ashamed of her father and felt no shame of her own in that belief. As long as she was stuck in Checcheri with him, she had to find ways to make the best of it; so, dinner alone it was.

She sat down and arranged her food on the table with the cloth. The cabbage was stuck to the bread, which wasn't stale any longer but overly moistened and falling apart. The quail was warm to the touch at best, and all the herbs it had been baked with had withered up and stuck to the cloth as it unraveled. Nevertheless, it was food, and she enjoyed it voraciously. She plucked and tore her way through it, not needing a fork for how soft it all was, and thought back on one incident that stuck out from her day. The run-in, physically, with the boy.

He had on fancy clothes like a scholar, except for his broken shoe. He was distracted and morose as well. She couldn't imagine what kind of stress he was put through to make him so inattentive that he not only ran into her but did so with enough force to topple over. She was only sturdy in the encounter because her training as a Porter made her walk with hard steps and unshaken confidence at a powerful pace. She had sure footing at all times, ensuring that the safety of even the most delicate package would not be compromised. Even if he had been carrying a boulder, she wouldn't have been put off-center.

Once her food was done, she bundled it up into its cloth and went to stow it in the bin with the rest of the day-to-day refuse. She went out behind the garage to place it in the bin and stood for a moment to admire the night sky and the perpetual twilight shimmer of the gas lamps and reflective miles of lit windows in the distance. Night never truly came in Checcheri. Someone somewhere always had to be awake for some reason. The only thing keeping her from being a Night Porter and making deliveries between waking hours was the training it required. The criminals and thugs of the day were paltry obstacles compared to the unspoken, but not underestimated, criminals of the night.

While she stood outside, she heard something familiar but out of place: the sound of wheels clattering back and forth and the clopping of an impatient horse inside. The garage was meant to be closed past a certain hour. Once the sun went down, there was nothing for her house to take in. Her father wasn't a Night Porter either; he was too old and timid to try. No packages were meant to come in until morning at the earliest, and yet it sounded like someone was inside. She had to investigate. It was her business, in a sense. Her father handled the contracts and exchanged the money, but whatever was happening, she would inevitably have to take control of it.

She snuck into the garage from the side entrance, where the room let out into the street for easy access, right next to her home's back door. She had gone that way many times before and knew that the door opened immediately to a narrow, walled-in stairway that went to the upper deck, which looked down on the wagons from above. She snuck up and stayed low in a crawl up the steps until her head was just barely peeking over the floor at the top of the stairs. No one was there; so, she kept herself low and edged just close enough to the railing to see down to the ground.

The carriage in the garage was loaded up with crates and barrels, and from Eidel's position, they looked unmarked. Without an approved crest from a Merchant Guild, no one could ship things in or out of the city, which meant it had to be local, but the cart itself looked foreign. It didn't have the same ergonomic design that she was accustomed to seeing. It was too long, past regulations. The wheels had metal studs on the inside of the rim that stuck out just a bit from the main spokes like it was built wrong or built dangerously on purpose.

Down below, she saw two figures talking, and when she relaxed her breathing enough, she could just hear them. One was a mystery and spoke in whispers, just out of sight in the shadow from where the lanterns lit the building. The other was her father, bearded, slumped over, and looking especially tired just standing in place. She kept crawling forward to eavesdrop. Whatever the deal was, she had to know its value.

"We can't cover for the cost of travel," her father said. Mr. Laun made plaintive motions with his hands, palms up, wrists forward, natural extensions of his bartering ways to show complacency and pleading with his apparently dissatisfied customer. The figure in question was cloaked from head to foot in midnight blue that twisted and wound up, revealing little of its form. Its face was hidden in darkness, aided by the shadows of its makeshift hood. "Not without the toll stamps from the main roads."

"We travel not," the figure said in a hissing whisper, a voice made by speaking while breathing in, "over watched roads. We must spurn the light to stay as shadows."

"I…. Okay," her father replied. He looked back at the carriage just as some of the items onboard began to jitter and move. The barrel lids unfastened, the crates slowly disassembled and quietly fell apart, and a darkness rose out like black water spilling from every container. Up stood a gathering of black-clad folks, shiny like a midnight lake, and the darkness that birthed them spilled out onto the floor and vanished. There was at least a dozen, as Eidel counted. She was more horrified by the emergence than curious and wasn't prepared to calculate with rationality the math required.

"The fare remains unadjusted from our discussion," the figure said. "The cargo, here, shall be dispersed. The wagon is, too, a form of the payment."

"I can't accept that," Mr. Laun said.

The figure drew in a ragged breath.

"Not ungratefully, mind you. I am grateful. It's a fine wagon. It can haul many things, but…but there are procedures I have to follow. I can't…I can't break every rule for you!" Mr. Laun exclaimed.

"You see the folly of the light," the figure said. It put a hand, armored in a gauntlet with sharp fingertips, on her father's shoulder, which stopped his objections along with his breath. "You see the worth of the dark. These rewards shall be a pittance after the final endeavor. We will not forget you when our mission is complete. The Laun family shall be the only one remaining once the darkness has taken hold."

"…yes," Mr. Laun finally muttered.

Eidel couldn't believe what she had heard. The short, sharp complacency against such an ominous and mysterious threat. She kept watching as the dark figures slowly departed from the wagon's back. Most of them were slim and featureless. Their armor was silent and shiny against their dark skin, like spandex that covered them from the neck down. They moved backward more comfortably and aptly than they did moving forward, when they went by creeping and slinking with their arms reaching outward.

One stood out, aside from the trader. That one was fully armored, its midnight skin nearly unseen, and despite the heavy plating sheathing its form, the being made no sound jumping down from the back of the wagon. Only the slight creaking of wheels that gave way beneath its weight made a sound, just loud enough to startle both of the Launs in their respective positions. The armored figure let out a long, deep breath that trailed slowly into a sick groan, like a weighted hinge on an old door that creaked more loudly the slower it was opened.

"Lord Victus," the trader said. The armored one, so named, turned his head, rounded with a crown of five sharp points like a clawed hand that reached up from his brow. His eyes shone deep blue under the dark cover of his visor. "By your honor, seal the contract with this lightborn man."

"Hmm," Victus hummed. He approached Mr. Laun, who retreated in tiny half-steps, seeming unable to run but obviously desperately wanting to. Victus took both hands to Mr. Laun's shoulders, then moved them up to his head and held him in place. Victus stood taller and stronger than her father, an ethereal being standing before the Guildsman. As Victus stared, his eyes went brighter until they flashed with a bolt of blue into Mr. Laun's eyes. The man yelped in a panic and lowered his voice immediately. He started to blink rapidly and reached his hands up to try to tend to his eyes. There was no pain. Once Victus released him, his body started to relax, and he looked up to his patron again.

"See as we see," Victus said, his voice a basal growl, like great stone dragging across the ground. "Watch for our sign." Victus made a motion in the air with his finger extended. It did nothing in plain sight, but Mr. Laun marveled at it, as his eyes could see the motions he made of an unknown character, as indecipherable to him as any language was. Two circles, one large below, one narrow above, and a pillar connecting them, which grew from the bottom, all made with a single unstopped motion.

"H-have a nice day, then," Mr. Laun said.

Victus turned and threw out his arm. His men, including the trader, ran for the rear garage door that let out into the street. Victus looked up to the walkway above briefly before he followed after them. Eidel had already seen enough. She left before they did, after her father was attacked. She had heard and seen all she needed at that point and raced back into the home to hide. What she knew was simple, and she ignored all the importance of the visitors or the nature of their being.

Her place in the Porter's Guild was now compromised due to this illegal trafficking, and it was all her father's fault. She kept herself locked in her small room, just big enough for her bed and her wardrobe, and fearfully mulled over what she would say to him in the morning. Her issues went far beyond normal disappointment. It was a matter of life and death....

4

Another day in Checcheri, another sprawl of workers and traffic moving by foot, by horse, and by cart along the winding ways. Baxter awoke once more, half-asleep with his hand already writing. His new dream revelation was far simpler than before and less ominous. He awoke to the sunlight and read before dressing.

One hundred sixty pages face down, 161 pages face up, 80 stitches, 50 braided wire, like the backside of a horse. Fell again. Fell Again?! Tower too tall, too tall, too tall.

The most sensible gibberish he'd ever produced. It made him crack a smile. All he could think about in his dreams was his Master's antics. His first binding work yesterday started with the heightened mood of his Master's impractical joking. He knew it wasn't intentional; the book was old enough to spill out its contents, but the follow-up was what kept Baxter interested. The chance to lightly and politely torment his Master over his slow, long "recovery" would have been funnier than staying to bat away his false injury. If he obeyed him then, he'd become the fool when he arrived with help into the tower where Lothan would no doubt be dancing or prancing around like he was twenty years younger.

He dressed himself like normal but slowed down once ready to clasp his hood. He was sighing more than normal, almost as a replacement for breathing. The work he was expected to do was not the same. It was different; not worse or better, but not what he'd expected. He'd gotten so used to the scribe work and the benefits that came with it of learning as he read that it felt like a setback to do something else instead. He could still read the work as he repaired it, but without the ease that came with copying it down. He learned better when his hand was moving to make words appear on pages and less well during slow, precise sewing work.

"All just a step at a time," Baxter said to remind himself. "Even Master has to bind books. He scribes, he custodes…. I can do it all too." Baxter nodded to himself in his mirror and went back to his nightstand on reflex. He already had his paper turned over and looked at the backside of it, where the previous night's ominous scrawlings were. He stared at the words all stretched out and biggened by his sleepy hand and focused hard on the one that was written in the smallest font but was still precisely readable. *Daemondimonium.* A word so odd, even reading it a day later gave him no context for it.

"I'll forget," Baxter said, "unless I have it." He folded up the page and slipped it into his breast pocket. He'd ask Master about it in the hopes of learning more, even if his words wouldn't reach him. Of all the people in all of the Vincian Empire, the Master Archivist was the likeliest person to know any word, no matter how foreign or vague it was. With that, Baxter went out, endured light jeering from his siblings again, and marched through the streets at a rapid pace to get to the Archive before anyone could call on him for duties. He had to get to Master Lothan before his work began, or he might not get the chance that day.

"Well, well," Derek said. He caught up with Baxter immediately using his long strides and strong legs. "Did you happen to read about exercise in a book, and now you're trying it out?"

Baxter was merely walking with speed, not hiking his legs up to run or jog, while Derek just looked like he was walking normally without strain.

"No harm in being early," Baxter replied.

"You've got it lucky, then," Derek said. "Did you hear about the First Western yet?"

"The old cathedral?" Baxter asked. The cathedral was one of the oldest built on the westernmost part of the city; its only windows faced the west, to endear a minor cult who worshiped at twilight so their hall would only receive the light of the setting sun. They believed the sun could rise from the west after it sank and in doing so would allow them to reverse the flow of time itself, which would enable them to travel into the past and correct grave mistakes. They were one of the loonier cults that had settled in Checcheri, second perhaps to the Tower Builders.

"It got sacked," Derek informed him.

Baxter slowed his pace a bit. The weight of the history he'd rehearsed to himself felt like walking against a stiff wind.

"Not too badly, at least," Derek added. "Work to be done, though. I never worked on a cathedral properly. Anything I ought to know about it first?"

"Nothing they won't tell you," Baxter said. "If any of the worshipers there are commissioning you, they'll likely ask you to attend their sunsetting service to hear their gospel. That's how most of the ministries recruit laborers to their congregations, sometimes with free food or drink as well."

"Shame for them, then," Derek said. "I don't have the attention for any more churches." Derek started a jog and easily left Baxter's side. He waved goodbye as he went on his way, too tall to disappear into the crowd until he was around a corner. It was just the motivation Baxter needed to keep his head up high. That, and the unfortunate recollection of yesterday's run-in with the girl. He had managed to repair his shoe, but it felt looser just thinking about it.

Once he reached the Archive, he was pleased to see it mostly under-occupied. The Custodians and Librarians were there, sorting through the many books stacked and layered high above that needed to be done that day. No one was guarding the central tower. It either meant the door was locked and the Master wasn't in, or he was in and no one wanted to bother him. Baxter, of course, had special permission to enter and was often entrusted—as one of the few trusted enough to enter the tower unbidden—to fetch Master Lothan for meetings and guests who came by.

It was locked, which shook up Baxter's plan a bit, but he was undeterred. His Master basically lived in the Archive. It seemed impossible to consider him absent. He stepped back and put his hands on his hips, looking around. He turned left, right, then stretched his neck up and saw something falling at him from above. He jumped a few steps back and watched a pile of paper descend from a walkway far above and then splash onto the ground where he had been standing.

"Ah, there you are!" Lothan's voice echoed from above. Baxter looked up and saw his Master leaning over the railing. "That one was on purpose. Bring those pages up to me and order them as you walk."

"I'm not catching you if you fall," Baxter called back.

"Very good to know," Lothan responded with a spry laugh. It was odd to see him out of the tower but not so odd to see him in great spirits when he was. The enormity of his work was a great burden on the old man. He didn't just scribe and bind old books; he had to translate them as well, as he was a master of many old languages. When he worked in the tower, he was closer to the morose and dreary nature of his responsibilities. When he was out and in the light with everyone else, he was far happier.

Baxter managed to sort the pages on his way up the stairs and across the walkways just in time to approach Master Lothan, who was flipping the pages of a small journal with one hand while holding the empty binding of Baxter's book with the other. While he wasn't watching, Baxter slipped his note out from his shirt and slid it into the assorted pages. His Master got the drop on him, so he would return the favor with his hanging query.

"It happens more than you think," Lothan explained. He pointed up quickly. "A book can fall from such a height that no part is left intact. The work of a Binder isn't just making old pages look new again with fancier covers. It's important."

"I can see why," Baxter replied. He handed the pages over. "Check them over, if you like."

"I very much would," Lothan retorted. He tucked the journal and the bindings underneath both of his arms and hugged them to his sides as he flipped through the pages one by one. Soon he came to the folded-up note between the papers and paused on it.

"Out of order?" Baxter asked, feigning ignorance.

Lothan gave him a stern look, seeing right through him, and pulled the note out. "What is this?"

"Oh!" Baxter exclaimed somewhat falsely. "That must have fallen out of my pocket when I was bent all the way over, using my back to lift and sort the papers out. Yes, that's mine. I meant to talk to you about it yesterday."

"I feel like this was not so much an accident," Lothan said, "as much as a desperate grab for my attention."

"I can't disprove your theory," Baxter replied.

"And what is it?" Lothan unfolded the note and looked it over. Baxter nodded and decided to drop his act and treat it with the seriousness that he believed it warranted—to prove to his Master that it wasn't a simple tit for tat but a deeply urged curiosity and an opportunity to learn.

"I take blank papers home with me," Baxter explained, "to practice writing, but also I keep one by my bed, and just before I fully wake each morning I write down everything I remember from my dreams. This is one that made me curious—"

"Fell again," Lothan read aloud, interrupting Baxter's explanation. His eyes perked up, and he heightened his tone. "*Fell again?!* Too tall, too tall, tall, tall—"

"The other side," Baxter instructed.

"Ah, of course." Lothan flipped the sheet over with a phony smile and looked at the other side. His expression changed immediately. The humor was gone. He became more intense and then looked upon the words with a held-back hatred.

"I don't recall ever knowing of such books," Baxter said, "related to the lore of the Abyss. And, that phrase, 'Daemondimonium.' I can't help but feel I may have seen or heard of it before. I wrote it out from a dream, after all. Like you saw, it's something stuck in my memory somewhere."

"Hmm, no," Lothan muttered quietly. He folded up the dream note and held it out for Baxter to take.

"No, what?" Baxter asked.

"I haven't heard of it," Lothan answered. "I think, perhaps, you read too much in the course of your work as a Scribe. Another fair reason to keep you as a Binder for some time to help your mind clear out of the unsettling histories you've read about."

"Well, hold on," Baxter began, but Lothan wagged the paper at him, and he took it and folded it back into his shirt pocket. Lothan wrapped up their conversation prematurely by stuffing the pages into the binding under his arm and pressing them together, ready to hand them off to Baxter once he was ready to listen.

"I'm sorry to judge, Master," Baxter said, "but you don't seem to have the attitude of a man who knows nothing. In fact, I dare to say, you seem to know something and have made it clear to keep me out of it."

"You read far too much," Lothan chastised with a small smirk. "But some knowledge can't be gained from a book. Including the understanding of when and where to best use one's knowledge. There are times and places for such things, dear boy, but you can't know them from just gleaning through texts all day."

"As you say," Baxter said, disappointed.

"Do you know why I am called the Learned?" Lothan asked.

"Because you have read over ten thousand books," Baxter answered with a rehearsed certainty.

"They increased the qualification," Lothan said, "to twenty thousand, cataloged and categorized, which I have also exceeded. But that name was earned earnestly and through the years of my life. And I did not read every random thing I could find. Those books were curated carefully for their value to society."

"And not like the books of fancy and myths that I read?" Baxter grumbled, impatiently assuming his Master's lesson.

Lothan raised his hand to stop his apprentice and lowered it slowly on top of the unbound book he held.

"Wisdom," he spoke, "is the knowledge of age. It is the knowledge of when it is proper to learn things and what is proper to learn. Without knowledge, the mind can be exposed to what it should not know or cannot learn. That is the quality of the Learned, and it is one that comes with age."

"...I see," Baxter replied. He was still disappointed, but the value of the lesson was worth more than his personal gripe.

Lothan patted the book like it was the boy's head and smiled to send him off. "Go on and fix that up first," he instructed. "The Binders are behind on their orders. They can use your talents best."

"Yes, Master," Baxter answered. He went off on his own, back down the sturdy stairs, while his Master remained up top to look down over the Archive.

The words Lothan had seen were still inside his head as if the scribbled ink of the note from the dream had sunken in and stained the backsides of his eyes. He looked down at Baxter, who was just recovering his pace and his attitude, with a solemn regret….

5

Daylight receded across the city of Checcheri. Families gathered for their meals after work. Fathers came home to waiting mothers; children went home to working mothers; children of families that couldn't subsist without both parents working did their best to tend the house as needed. Everyone was grateful for a day to end in peace, as peace had been commonplace for centuries.

Baxter left the Archive a changed lad. He went in with little expectation over being a Binder and left far more confident and resounding in the utter lack of appeal it carried for him. He was good at it, so much so he found it easy, but it left him little time to read. He spent most of his day contemplating his place in the Archive while he showed up his seniors, who disparaged him for being such a young and over-favored apprentice. The work came so easy that he didn't have to think about it; he just bound the books and wished he could read them.

It made his march home take on a melancholic mood. He crossed the main street and began his descent toward the Festival Quarter to a home of raucous celebrations by his brothers over not dying yet again in their fevered day of hard and heavy lifting. The rest of the clerks and workers of the Archive filtered out one by one after saying their goodbyes and offering their prayers that the books endure another solemn night untouched and unpilfered.

The Master, however, stayed behind. As he was the Master of the great Archive, he was the closest to it, and one of the elite few permitted to remain inside once the sun went down. His work often took him deep into the night and long into the great shelves and rows in search of hidden tomes to fulfill the requests of the great patrons who supported the hallowed halls in exchange for knowledge. That was the true duty of the Master: to perform every job within the Archive himself and complete full restorations overnight.

Along with him was a nighttime assistant, a servant loaned from a higher house that sponsored the Archive. She spent her time studying the simple books to learn to read for her lord's benefit. Young Marley, with her bonnet-covered hair and big round reading glasses, scanned her way slowly through a book on the ground floor while Lothan worked far above. Just as he began a trek downward with a heavy tome in his hands, another figure entered the Archive, invited in on their own whim and with an entourage behind them.

"I'm sorry," Marley said. "The Archive is not accepting any tenants, donors, or perusals after sundown. If you'd like to—" She looked up from her book in awe at the spectacle. A group of clergymen, about eight in total, with dark robes hiding their faces, stood in the walkway of the lobby just against the open threshold where the old cathedral's hallowed grounds ended and the grand library began.

One of them stepped forward and unhooded herself. She was an older woman, very elegant, with cosmetics that hid her true age with a smooth veneer of polished, silky, skin-toned foundation. It made her a shade paler than normal. Her hair was spread out from her head in the shape of an open-bottomed pastry, perfectly round just off the top of her head and then spread out in many dainty bouncing curls around her neck. Like her head itself was wearing a gallant bell-shaped gown.

"Is Master Lothan in?" she asked with a sing-songy voice. Though she carried gentle tones, Marley felt like the request was anything but. It had the same noble air of rhetoric she was trained to infer meaning from as sincere, a question not meant to be answered with words but fulfilled by action.

"Uh, may I ask who would summon him?" she inquired.

The woman just smiled kindly, lips wrinkling the deep-red makeup on them like wax paper.

Marley nodded in response and excused herself to go and run for Master Lothan—who just then touched ground and huffed out with a heavy book under his arm. It was large, thick, and very archaic, from an era where all papers were thick as well as wide and written with large print.

"Master Lothan," Marley breathed, "someone wishes to see you."

"Hmm," he grunted. He looked around and observed the descending darkness of the night that encroached upon the shielded candles that lit the walkways above. "That's unfortunate for them. It's too dark for me to see anything. And what good is it to be seen if one cannot see as well to return the favor?"

"Sir?" she prompted.

"Tell them I'm blind," he commanded. "I've become very sick, very suddenly ill, and it's cost me my everything, my health and my mind, and I cannot see them at all and to come back tomorrow."

Marley stood confused, and in her absence of duty at the door, the mysterious guests entered of their own accord. She stood between her Master and the odd lady, nervously glancing between them as their eyes seemed to meet.

"Oh," Lothan said. "Very well." He patted Marley softly on the shoulder. "Thank you, Miss Marley. I...*we* will attend to our business in the Hall of Restrictions."

"How fitting," the lady said.

"Well, it is a place where sensitive words are painted over thickly so as not to be read again," he said with a very visible glance toward her face. "I'd say it is…fitting."

The other hooded figures stifled laughs and deep chuckles. The woman rolled her eyes and followed Lothan as they all departed deeper into the cathedral's hidden halls of former worship. The Restrictors and Rewriters were tasked in their ritualistic room, a private chamber meant for group confessions, to fix the words in books that had fallen out of style or lost their meaning through changing times at the request of those who had been meant to read them. It was a place of silence, where words came to die.

When they all entered, sliding across the floor like shadows, Lothan closed the door and stood nearest to it, assuming the head of the gathering while the lady stood opposite and assumed her own type of control.

"Let us begin," she spoke, "the meeting of the Gazers."

"Let us see," the rest uttered in prayer, "and understand."

"You got here fast," Lothan mentioned. "I barely whispered into the wind, and you assembled the same night."

"You had an advantage," she replied, raising her hand up. "From that tower, words spoken could reach any ear."

"That's what it's good for," he said. He hoisted up the book and moved to a nearby podium to set it down. The hooded man nearest shuffled away to give him space. "Come and look upon this," he instructed. The lady stepped close, though not quite close enough to read. The rest all beheld the book in an uneven cluster while Lothan flipped the pages. The text was big and squared, written by a hand without concern for aesthetic or design, focused only on communing the full breadth of their knowledge as fully as possible.

Every few pages were illustrations, drawn by a practiced but still unclear hand. Beasts worth recognizing were warped and exaggerated, and all of them had a similar face, like an angry, round-featured, hunting dog. Even depictions of great crawling lizards, birds that preyed on men, and other monstrosities bore that same face.

"Not a high-talent piece of art," one of the figures, an old man, noted.

"Aside from that," Lothan commented, "it's all true. This book represents the oldest known Living Lore of the Old World, from the region of Ishma, near the Undermountains."

The group stood in awe. The woman stepped forward and looked over the writings as Lothan flipped through to a much later page. "Why now?" she asked. "Is this book so easily opened by the Master Archivist?"

Lothan paused to collect his thoughts. He looked up at her as she awaited his response, and he struggled to find the one that would meet her expectations. He only had one to give, though.

"The Contract of Old," he said, "is nearing its end." The rest of the group went into silence and exchanged worried looks. "You've heard it, surely.

You, Master Trimius, and you Master Mashash." He glanced at the two men in turn. "You've heard of the war. Far to the east, a force grows. It emboldens each day. It tears up the land and feasts on destruction. A force of war unlike any other, with all the ethics and mercy of a great storm that ruins the crops and breaks apart buildings, led not by a single man but a high ideal. The Horde of Shadows, I believe they are called."

"They have many names," the one addressed as Mashash, with a thick neck and a squared, gray beard, confirmed. "Though they see their charge as far more holy and righteous than we do. We see a rampaging monstrosity, a horde of bandits brought together by the words of a long-passed warlord, propelled by his message to unite and sow chaos in his name."

"Their work is heretical," another old man said. "They are deifying a corpse foreign to the lands they trample. They are working against the path of life itself."

"Rumors have spread," a woman with an accent that favored Rs and sharp, stiff vowels, spoke, "that a new contract has already been forged and that the valley in Ishma has already come under their occupation. They have seized the Skymouth. They have invaded the Mount Abyss."

"That cannot be possible," the pale lady said.

"Madam Suttwood is right," Lothan said. "Mount Abyss is a place where only death exists. It is the reverse and antithesis of the world we know. None can traverse it unless they have a contract with one of its Walkers. The Shades do not tolerate the living easily. They may favor one life, brought in sacrifice, with a will strong enough to shift their dark wills, but not an army."

"Could it be," began Master Trimius, a fully bald and shaved man with a long and stiff face that showed the bones of his skull more than the muscles of his flesh, "that the one they worship and have consecrated so was the one who forged this new contract? If so, any aim this army has would be shared by the Shades."

"How do you know this?" Madam Suttwood asked.

Lothan nodded slowly, then quickly. "It occurred in a dream," he said, "that my apprentice had."

"Your apprentice?" she repeated with mild shock. "Is it…?" She pointed toward the door, through the wall, and in the direction of the entryway.

"No, not her," Lothan said. "The boy is more…knowledgeable. Curious. Deathly so. He records his dreams with some accuracy and was able to know the titles of books that we ourselves took to hiding for the safety of the Archive. Books he never should have known existed. Including this one here, which only I know where to find and what its true name is."

"Is that not coincidental?" she asked. "Does he not read the books he works on each day?"

"The name of this tome," Lothan said, fingers pressed onto the unmoving, stiff page, "is a word this very room is dedicated to removing. It has been enlisted as a cursed word that all written works of any importance have henceforth been barred from containing. The gravity of him knowing it is incredibly pressing, and the fact that he dreamed of

Shades walking along the light and of the Mount Abyss itself…I fear, or rather, I have acknowledged the distinct possibility that the Living Lore has entered a Revision."

"A Revision?!" one man exclaimed. Lothan's proclamation drove the group into a mild fluster. Madam Suttwood put out her arms and tried to calm them. She reached for the book and flipped through the pages to the back. In one of the final lengths of writing, a depiction of a massive dark mountain was drawn with such heavy ink it stained through to the other side of the page. There, a rune was carved into the paper, scraped in with the dried tip of an inkless pen. A circle below that surrounded the mountain base, the mountain itself, and a circle above just under its peak, all drawn with a single pen-stroke as a single continuous shape.

"If this is true, and your apprentice has envisioned the Mount Abyss and the Contract of it, what must he do?" Madam Suttwood asked.

"He?" Lothan repeated. He reached over and closed the book. Its weight caused it to fall right into his hands, and he cradled it under his arm. "He has more important things to do with his youth. He isn't ready to become a Gazer. He's still just a boy."

"You act like he's your son," Madam Suttwood insisted. "Is he not the apprentice you brag about so often?"

"I thought he was your grandson by secret," Master Mashash chimed in. "I even looked into it, but no, he's a simple common boy. He learned to read quite young, but his family is poor and labor-driven."

"The prophecies do speak," the oldest man said, "that innocence shall shine like light from the darkest shadows under the mountains, but that naivety and ignorance will blind all who look on and shall create a hell of light that will rival the fearful dark."

"And I'd like," Lothan said, "to not let that happen. He's exactly at the point of naivety right now, and curiosity the likes of which could shift rooms and rock buildings. If he enacted Living Lore now, with such little training—"

"Then I will train him," Madam Suttwood decided. "As the Loremaster of this circle, of we

Gazers, I can teach the boy the method and power of the incantations of mythical history."

Lothan held his book tight. "You're just jealous my apprentice likes what he does," he mumbled.

"Lothan," she said, foregoing his title of Master, "do not forget our sacred duty. For we who gaze into the Abyss must be ever prepared for it to gaze back. Do you believe you can go alone to revise the Living Lore, to forge a new contract? Is the prophecy about you, whose innocence has been lost and naivety dead for decades?"

"No," he admitted. "But Baxter will not be included either. I shall control the book for now. In the meantime, the Horde of Shadows should be monitored and deterred from leaving the Primal World."

"The Living Lore out there is weak," one of the Gazers said. "What methods can we use to deter them that have not already failed?"

"We have new books," Lothan said, "on the recent trends of rifling and other masterwork gun-making techniques. If they become popular among the nobility, commissions for guns may experience a spike in the bordering states."

"And I suppose that's my job," another man said with a sigh.

"Now, then," Lothan said as he reached for the door, "let us see no more of each other for another four or five weeks, please. And when we do, let it be before evening."

The Gazers adjourned and left the Archive. Lothan remained in his tower, high up in a floor dedicated to the storage of precious works far from any hands that might try to pilfer them. He laid the book down and stared at it as if it were staring him down first to make him flinch. The *Daemondimonium*. The Land of Many Daemons. The compendium of the knowledge of one mad traveler who explored the Old World's myths in the age when they were closer to reality than anything else. Explorer of the unseen world of daemons, monsters, and shades.

Walker onto the Mount Abyss....

6

As the evening came, dwindling all illumination in Checcheri down to lamplight and window candles lining the streets in uneven patterns, the hard workers who toiled in daylight made their returns home to rest and relax through the night. Tomorrow would be another day, one of constant work and even more laborious effort to eke out their living in the world of royal standards.

Derek minded none of it. Not the hierarchy or his place in it. He had worked hard and intended to live hard thereafter—by first sleeping hard once he found his way home. He was a strong young man, far stronger than most. His father had been strong as well, and he used his own strength to support his mother as well as himself. His arms were taut and flexed from the effort, and his back was arched back with confidence. No matter where he walked, he did so with long strides that occupied the road as his territory where no one could cross his path. No one he didn't know.

When he saw someone he was acquainted with, one of his distant co-workers or his few and fair friends, he would approach them with the rumble of a runaway cart. That evening, as the secret meeting was being held within the Archive, Derek spotted Baxter on his way through the streets and approached him from the front.

"Hey, Baxter!" he called out. "Did your eyes wear the rest of your body out reading all day?" He saw that Baxter didn't respond and was just staring at the ground ahead as he moved, totally vacant and distracted.

Derek stopped and moved out of Baxter's way, then caught up with just a few more steps to give him a light, polite shake of his shoulder. It was enough to nearly throw Baxter's hood up over his head.

"Oh, hello," Baxter finally replied. "Where'd you come from?"

"From in front of you," Derek said, a bit worried. Baxter saw his friend's expression and rubbed under his eyes. "You didn't really get tired just from reading all day, did you?"

"No," Baxter said. "No, I didn't get tired reading."

"That's good for you then," Derek said. "If I got this tired hauling stone and pulling rope at the cathedral, they'd dock my pay. You're lucky if they let you work in such a state."

"Well, I wasn't working like this all day," Baxter explained. "I really only got tired after being told that I was too young to appreciate any of the books that we were repairing and how I shouldn't even be able to read at all, peasant-class this, waste-of-sight that."

"You get their names?" Derek asked. He smoothed the knuckles of his fist in his calloused palm. "Pick them out of a crowd?"

"It's not that bad," Baxter said. He went on his way, but Derek followed, insisting with his constant grinding fist that his way could work. "I'm one of the youngest workers there. It's just me and a servant girl from a noble house who's only there as an asset for a noble sponsoring the work. Not that anyone treats her wrongly for it, but it's just…I…."

"She cute?" Derek asked. Baxter rocked his head back and forth indecisively—then uncontrollably as

Derek shook him again. He shrugged him off finally, which gave Derek a reassured smile. "C'mon, you've got to start keeping your head up for cute girls, yeah? Noble's servant is a pretty good hitch-up, I think."

"That's depressing," Baxter said. "That I'm still counted as lower than a noble's servant."

"Well, at least you're not a district house servant," Derek reminded him, "or a debtor servant. Or one of the other kinds of servants working around. I have to work with mostly servants, and they're all slackers."

"They must lack ambition," Baxter said sardonically. "Imagine that, being stripped of your freedom to live and not having the motivation to work."

"They'd be happier if they worked harder," Derek countered. "Pay their debts easier."

Baxter sighed. Derek's straightforward sincerity, compared to his own arduous learnedness in all things, was only rarely frustrating. It had been an already frustrating day, and Derek's inanity had worked Baxter up to a boiling point of derisive conversation.

"If working hard mattered," Baxter began, "then you'd be a noble, but you're not because you weren't born in the right section of the city. Look." He pointed up toward the peak of Checcheri, the Mount of Brick as it was called, almost entirely manmade extensions of the hill on which the city was founded. It rose up on the grade higher and higher to the Royal Quarter far above, like the crest of a rolling mountain in the distance. "You have to be born in a house up there to have real freedom. And look where we are now—where *I* am!" Baxter pointed down the Festival Quarter street. Some people were outside, as were some chickens pecking away in the middle of the road. "I'm sorry," Baxter sighed. "It's not like me to get worked up like this."

"I know," Derek said. He was completely accepting of Baxter's outpouring of frustration. He knew, at least, that his friend never had hatred for him when he corrected him. He just wasn't always patient enough to endure Derek's constant questions.

"I'm still thinking," Baxter said, "about my duties and the Master's work. I came to him with an honest query I hoped he could solve. I thought he and I had enough closeness, as far as apprenticeships go, that he would encourage me to learn as much as I could. I suppose I should get used to being turned away from things I want, though. Even if I make my way to the Master Archivist title, I'll still be treated like a servant by those above me."

"I didn't know books were worth so much business," Derek said. He looked back over his shoulder and up the street and noticed something stirring around. Figures moved like tricks of light, casting shadows from the flickering of a candle's light, but no light source or nearby things were out and moving. The only other creature up that far was a cat that went shock-still when it saw what Derek had seen.

"Well, I shouldn't bore you with the seniority strife at the Archive," Baxter sighed. "How does your work make you feel as a person?" Baxter waited for a chipper, ethically sound response, but Derek was distracted. He turned to see by what and just missed the disappearance of shadows slinking through the streets at the end of the block.

"Uh? Sorry," Derek said. "I thought I saw…something."

"It's not a nice place," Baxter reiterated. "But it is home."

"And, yeah," Derek said as if a thought he just had was the start of a conversation he forgot to mention, "why not just go in and learn? Isn't the Archive, like, open?"

"Not at night," Baxter said.

"Well, neither is the cathedral in repair," Derek pointed out, "but if a man wants a place to sleep without fear of retribution, he can bring a lantern, tap a hammer to the wall, and pretend to be working for a while to sleep indoors if he's got no better option."

"Do you also work with criminals?" Baxter asked.

"A cathedral's a cathedral." Derek shrugged. "They're supposed to be places of gathering and worship, sort of, and a place full of books ought to be a place of learning, I'd consider."

"Yes, but they can't be staffed all day," Baxter answered. "If they were, I'd be the one forced to staff it, probably."

"Then why not just go in right now?" he suggested. "Find that book that's aching your mind to be read and read it! Say you had work and fell asleep getting it done."

"How is the cathedral project actually going?" Baxter asked.

Derek chuckled.

"No, I'm not breaking into the Archive, one of the most important places in all of Checcheri, just to spend all of my evening hours through midnight and on 'til morning looking through thousands of books for a title that might not be real."

"Why not?" Derek asked. His sincere, honest inquiry put Baxter off-guard. He knew why he shouldn't, but in his mind, he didn't have a solid answer as to why he couldn't. He very much could. He knew all the side entrances and could navigate the halls and walkways even in the dark. It wouldn't matter if someone else was there; they'd get lost trying to apprehend him. He wouldn't even have to steal the book. He knew the cathedral was stocked with priest quarters on the upper floors that were converted into reading rooms. No one would look in there for him. Even just for a few hours, for one day, he could read.

"Well," Baxter began, then continued with a sigh, "I'd just never thought of that."

"It's a good thing you know me, then." Derek patted Baxter on his back, the force of which propelled him a few steps forward each time. "I used to sneak onto job sites all the time just to hang out with the other lads while they drank."

"And you were never caught," Baxter said with false pride.

"Oh, yeah, I was," Derek replied with a proud, nostalgic smile. "Didn't take the fall for it, but those drunken fools sure did."

"Huh," Baxter huffed. He looked back down the street. He could see, and nearly hear, his own house full of rowdy celebration. Loud, distracting cheers of drinks and celebrations over whatever job they were doing and whatever pay they hadn't quite earned. A house he was sad he belonged to. He looked away, over the rooftops, and toward the Archive instead and felt more whole gazing at it. He also saw some shapes, not quite birdlike, more like cats moving across the roofs until they vanished into shadows.

"All right," Baxter said. "May as well. If Master is going to keep secrets from me, I'll start my training as a Librarian and find this mysterious compendium myself."

"Yeah!" Derek exclaimed.

Baxter pointed a wagging finger at his friend. "And you can carry it."

"Ye…aw, I've messed this all up, haven't I?" Derek asked.

"Well you've done this all before," Baxter explained, "and I haven't! I need a guiding hand to help me criminalize myself for the first time. I want it to go right like yours did!"

"You're too smart for your own good, I say," Derek complained.

He was a good man with a helpful soul, and Baxter knew it. He didn't even have to put on a pleading look. He already knew that in Derek's heart was not just a will but an urge to help.

"Well, go on and lead me there," Derek insisted.

Baxter nodded and started walking back the way he came. The two boys went through town together, a strange pair to pass through the mostly empty streets, one in scholarly robes and the other with a shirt that was more sweat stains than original color. Derek walked with a hunch and kept his hands trousered, exaggerating his mood over being tricked into helping.

While they walked, yet more figures were out and about. Some rare, infrequent citizens with nightly jobs were moving out to start their working hours after many other houses had already gone to sleep. Day laborers and Merchant Guild workers perused the town from the edges of the Festival Quarter where all the bars and taverns were located to line the second main street from hill to castle gate.

Shadows also swept over the roofs and through alleys, unseen and unbelievable. Distinctly human in all but their movements. They woke and stunned every animal that saw them, as their instincts stirred them into stasis, for they knew what walked before them was death. The Shades were moving, and all of them were converging toward the center of the town at the middle of the hill, where the lower sections were separated by a long, flat round where the cathedrals of old were built up high. Among them, moving silent as the breeze and with long strides was the dreaded Victus. Each step of his gentle walking propelled him to another roof until the houses ended and the sky-reaching, vaulted ceilings began.

The Shades stalked the night and evaded all light up to the neighboring cathedral's roof. The length of the roads away was lit by the gaslit posts that lined the main road of the street. The two boys crossed the way and went for the Archive, with its paramount tower reaching high over its surroundings, many stories beyond any other building in the middle of the sprawling city. The Shades all breathed irregularly; every drag of breath was a hiss and a snarl that ended in a *snap* sound as if they were biting the very air away to swallow it in chunks.

Victus observed the boys from above with his pale blue eyes beneath his clasped armored crown. The pair moved to a side door, hidden in darkness, and fumbled with it until the larger of the two used his strength to force the lock with a quick twist of the handle and lifted the heavy, unserviceable door so it wouldn't screech along the ground below it. The other hooded boy went in first, and they both left the way open as they entered.

Victus let out an ethereal sound like rocks grinding. It prompted the rest of the phantasmal troupe to move and crawl down the walls like so many massive insects, all backward and facing outward. He, meanwhile, stepped off and walked gently down as his body glided through the air. When he landed, he faced the opening in the Archive but turned around with glaring eyes to the brightened street.

He did not see the third who was present, a curious and hard-headed girl who was bundled up in a shawl for cover who took to hiding behind the wall of one of the last houses in the row down the street. She followed the Shades on their excursion to see what wicked plans they had. She had to know what risk her father had put them both into for these apparently sinister and most assuredly unnatural beings. She saw them all enter the Archive, a place she'd never been and had only seen on her fast marches past as a Porter. But she knew what it was, and with so many strangers surrounding it, she could only assume great evil was afoot....

7

The Archive was, oddly, lit up inside. Candles burned in special wax-catching sconces throughout the walkways and around every hall. Despite the presence of flames combined with uncountable tons' worth of flammable paper, the danger of anything burning down was considerably rare. Even at night when the fires continued by candle, gas, or via moonlight through the windows in the roof, the Archive was never truly empty. That was why it was imperative for Baxter and Derek to sneak their way to the upper levels.

After one half-step onto the stairs, Baxter had to retreat. He could feel a creak about to happen. He stood balanced on one heel while Derek ducked his impractical frame down, as his head darted around all over the place. He'd never seen so many books before. He'd never even opened one.

"Hey," Derek muttered. His voice, set against the dead silence of the Archive, made Baxter jump slightly. "I take it back. This place is neat."

"Take what back?" Baxter whispered even lower than Derek could.

"That this place is for stick arms that can't lift nothing heavier than stale bread," he explained. "You know, not in a mean way."

"Just be careful up the stairs," Baxter whispered. He took a step toward the edge of the step and managed to ascend without making any noise. Derek did the same. Though his heavier frame made the wood creak out regardless, he kept very quiet with slow steps that modulated his pressure carefully. They reached the top of the first walkway, and Baxter took a look at the labels of the shelves built around the tower's base.

"This thing," Derek mentioned quietly, "is more impressive up close. I see it all the time, never bothered to come in and give it a look."

"It's hollow inside," Baxter said as he ran his finger along the rim of the shelf. "Nah, not here. These all start with J."

"A tower that big is empty?" Derek asked with a hushed exclamation, just a little too loud for a whisper. Baxter pumped his hand to stop him.

"It's got rooms within it," he corrected. "It's just a tower."

"It's the most talked-about engineering feat among the Mason's Guild," Derek explained. "The fact that they made it so tall in the first place calls for equipment that they can't even design and never existed. And it's at an angle—did you know that? If you put a level to it at the right place it tilts just a little to the east, but not the exact east. It's southeast-ish."

"I didn't know that," Baxter mentioned. "One of the books inside probably describes why they made it like that, though. If we find it, I'll read it to you."

"Really?" Derek whispered. The childlike, hopeful wonder in his voice over the prospect of being read a book, of wanting to learn something presented in a book, made Baxter sincerely happy.

"That's another mission," he said. "Our first order of business is finding the book I need."

"Right," Derek said. He followed after him, a story and a half off the ground, on the hunt for the proper section his desired book would be in. If it existed at all, a copy of it would be housed in the Archive, and the taciturn denial of Master Lothan told Baxter that it absolutely must be here somewhere. He just hoped that his Master hadn't found it first, since infiltrating the tower itself would be far too risky.

Meanwhile, on the ground floor, only one other person was attendant to the Archive at night. The servant girl of noble employ, Marley. She was on a very late shift, from late afternoon approaching evening and all the way through until morning. Then she would return home to rest in a darkened room, wake up just after noon, and tend to household chores while answering her lord's questions about the goings-on inside the vaulted cathedral walls. Her latest report made her anxious to leave early if she could. The happenings she observed and listened in on seemed too important not to share with someone immediately.

While she waited at the desk, passing her time absentmindedly reading some tome of mystical, falsified adventures from a distant shelf a Custodian or Librarian would have to find for her, she missed the many entries that came in far behind her through the abbey entrance in the back. She didn't notice a thing, not a creak of stairs or the far-off hushed whispers of hidden conversations. She did notice a light go out nearby. Just around the corner from it was nothing but darkness, and the light's sudden absence turned the pillar before the side halls much darker.

She picked up her light at the desk and walked it over to reignite the missing light. As she did, a hand emerged from the shadows—as if it were indeed part of the darkness and had stretched out of its own accord—and clamped over her mouth. She dropped the candle just as it illuminated the form the hand belonged to but not enough to see anything beyond a humanoid shape. Before the brass holder hit the floor, another hand reached out from below, as if its owner was crawling on its belly, and caught it by the looped handle. Then, it turned the holder upside down and snuffed the light against the floor.

All that was left before her was darkness. The hands blended into it and joined a massive, unseen figure, a being of mysterious and immense darkness with many bodies, heads, and separate arms, a clustered form that she could not make out beyond the strain of lost breath and her tears of fear. Then a light came from it, dim and blue. Another joined it, side by side, the distance and shape of two eyes. A more solid shadow moved through the tangle of forms and laid its hand over the one that still covered her mouth. Her muted screams were stopped as the dark figure applied pressure to her, and the glow in his eyes intensified.

Marley's struggles stopped. Her arms went down, and she was gently lowered onto her feet. She slumped over and backed away, off-balance but not falling. The dread hand of Victus let her go. His fingers pricked a glowing trail of symbols in the air, all blurring together and left unseen by all but Marley's blank, sunken eyes. When she saw them, her body moved at his command and walked to the opposite side of the entryway. She reached up, fearless of pain, and squelched another hanging candle out with her fingers. It singed her slightly with a hissing fizzle, but her mind was not her own any longer, and she did not feel the injury.

The Shades had infiltrated the Archive. One impatient shadow moved toward the tower in a crawl, but as soon as its body entered the light it went from a malleable, gas-like entity to the solid, lanky-bodied form it had assumed before. The light warped it into solidity, and it reacted with a long, gasping wheeze of pain before it retreated into the absence of light where its body returned to a lingering mass of floating eyes, like stars peering through a thin cloud.

Victus traced more orders for Marley, and she shambled off to obey. Her skin turned gray starting from her eyes and pouring outward over her body. The veins underneath turned black. Her soul was gone; her body moved with a purpose that was not her own. It was not to say whether she was alive or dead, but she was not able to resist the beckoning lights of the terrible Shade Lord's hand.

The fires went out, one by one, as fast as the girl could drag her sleepwalking feet around, creating a path of darkness toward the base of the tower. Meanwhile, up above, Baxter and Derek continued their search, completely unaware of the silent invasion taking place below. As they searched, Baxter would notice books of interesting subjects and hand them off for Derek to carry. He had four large tomes cradled in one arm and six smaller books in two stacks of three spread across the other.

"Mate," Derek whispered, "I'm fine to haul all of these, but isn't it a bit much to read through? I thought we'd only be here a hot minute to find that thing you were told not to think about."

"Supposing I don't find it," Baxter said, "I want to make the most of this. I'd read something while I'm here, at least."

"Just how easy is it to read that you can have all these for one night?" Derek asked.

"Oh, no," Baxter said. "I can handle maybe one, or two if they're brief. No one will know they're missing if we put them on a Custodian's cart. Their entire existence in the Archive is to shuffle books from one place to another without ever taking a break or wondering why."

"So, they're stonies?" Derek asked. "Ones who carry stones up the scaffolds for masons to lay and work around?"

"Are you a stoney?" Baxter asked.

"On even days," he answered. "Odd days, I'm a rigger. Build up and put down scaffolds."

"Are you really even building a cathedral then?" Baxter asked.

"Rigging is an essential part of the process," Derek retorted with defensive conceit.

Baxter smirked and looked around. He noticed, finally, that the lights below were going out, one after another. "That's odd," he said.

"Lights-out time?" Derek asked.

"It'll be a chore to leave at this rate," Baxter realized. "Let's get back down while there's still any light to see with."

"You didn't find what you were looking for?" Derek asked.

Baxter clenched a fist and sighed. He'd scanned the shelf he thought it would be on: D for the letter, cross-referenced against the section handling matters related to Old World Lore and Geographic Texts, but he had found nothing. No journal, tome, or encyclopedia matched the name he'd written from his fevered dreaming state. The *Daemondimonium* was simply missing.

"It's fine," Baxter said with an acceptance of defeat in his smile. "At least we did this. Didn't just fall on my bed and moan myself to sleep like usual."

"Yeah," Derek confirmed. "And you got exercise walking all these stairways."

"What will it take for you to acknowledge the physical demands of this job?" Baxter asked, just a bit frustrated.

Derek had just opened his mouth to answer when they both heard the rattling of a door. Derek couldn't move to check below because his hands were stacked full of books. Baxter leaned over the railing and peered to the ground where the shadows all gathered.

Then they both heard a startling clatter. The door to the tower had been forced open. It locked from the inside, and the act of unlocking it would not make noise at that scale. Moreover, what worried Baxter was that it had been locked. Master Lothan was one of the few people with the key to enter freely. He wouldn't have to push the door open just to gain access to his own tower.

Then he saw the entrants: intruders who hid in the darkness. They skulked in one by one, some entering the dim lighting of the tower single-file while other vague shapes spread out into the dark of the Archive rows. It was an outright invasion, a burglary of a level that made Baxter's petty, late-night "book-loaning" seem inconsequential.

"That doesn't look right," Derek whispered. Baxter tapped on the banister nervously and broke out into a hopping, careful jog to the nearest stairs. Derek followed, still cradling books, making much more noise. They could both already hear the chaos inside the tower, the clattering of many feet heading up the stairs, and the breaking of furniture inside the lower floors.

Baxter reached the edge of the steps, but the way down was darkened. Halfway down, he couldn't see any of the stairs past the absence of light. "Come on!"

Baxter hissed, raising his voice from a whisper to a hushed tone of panic.

"I'm going," Derek answered hastily. He shifted himself to keep the books in his arms. "Stoney-ing is hard when you have to rush."

"Leave them behind," Baxter instructed. "This is more important than—"

Before he reached the end of the stairs, he heard voices from within the tower. Some hisses, some throaty sounds like a cat retching in the open street, and then a grand voice with a deep, booming tone elocuting words unheard and unknown with great force through the vertical stone halls of the grand pillar. As the voice reached its apex, a light built up. From an upper floor too high above to determine its level, a flood of light traveled out and flashed into the room below, illuminating the lower floor like the morning sun breaking through drawn curtains.

At that moment, as brief as lightning in the sky, Baxter saw the shapes of suffering creatures, shaped like men but warped and contorted. Bulbous arms, swollen backs, wide, beast-like faces with fanged mouths and white eyes like stars against a dark sky. Visions that evoked a sense of familiar dread within him, a dread that caused his hand to clutch shut with fingers pressed together like he was holding a pen. A fear he felt from his dreams that had earlier etched their way onto paper. *No bodies or light.* Shades.

"Was that an explosion?" Derek asked.

Baxter dismounted the stairs immediately and ran for the tower opening. Derek ran after him and lowered the books to the ground in front of the open archway. He stacked them up immediately, like a tiny, flimsy pile of bricks. Not exactly a stopper for anything robust enough to kick down a door but a small deterrent nonetheless. It was all he could think to do in the confusing darkness. His first time in the Archive and his first opportunity to be surrounded by books, and it had become a deadly struggle against phantasmal burglars.

As the boys rushed in, the Shades reconvened outside and surrounded a single target. The dim blue glow of Victus's eyes brightened until it compensated for the snuffed candles. The sharp blue light continued building until the candles relit, their flames blue with shadowy black at the wick instead of bright white. He groaned out in a deathly voice and stared into the still, dark opening of the tower. The Shade Lord's eyes narrowed; his blue eyes shimmered with repulsion. Their assault had been rebuked, but their target was still present. They just had to wait it out….

8

Baxter hiked up the stairs faster than he ever had before in his life. The potent mixture of his emotions—the high that came with his own lawless intrusion and terror after witnessing the presence of the unknown assailants—pushed him to a level of panic he hadn't thought his mind capable of experiencing. He kept himself focused, dedicated to a single directional push of effort. Something was at the top of the stairs in the upper rooms of the tower and he had to reach it. Something, or someone, had been attacked up in the tower, and something had happened that made the attack cease. He had to find out what had occurred in the tower. He had to find his Master.

"Baxter!" Derek called. For once, he was the one falling behind. He wasn't as prone to the rush of excitement in a panic, and his heavy body was harder to push up the stairs. Baxter didn't stop for him and Derek could tell why. He kept going onward and upward after Baxter's charge, panting deeply.

Baxter ascended past the highest point he'd ever been to and still saw no sign of his Master nor even one of the creatures that had rushed in before. They had vanished. The light seemed to have chased them away. It was just like his dream script, like the old tales and myths he'd read. Creatures like living shadows that could emerge from any darkness but feared the light as it could erase their very existence away. But nothing he knew could make light so bright and powerful that it reached from the near top of the tower all the way to the bottom.

Each floor they both passed seemed less disheveled. The lower floors had evidence of damage done, shelves torn down, and books scattered to the floor, but the higher up the invaders got, the less distracted they had apparently become. Perhaps they had been more focused on climbing—or perhaps chasing—at that point to get to their target.

"Master!" Baxter shouted. "Master, are you here?!"

"Mister Book Master!" Derek shouted, out of breath. "We're here, but we're not with them, okay?"

Baxter finally reached the top floor, the highest level accessible. The rest of the tower was sealed from below, and the mad priests who built it had continued its construction even after they had been locked away through means no man had discovered since. The floor beneath was a windowed observation platform. From there, the flash of light was seen all over the city, and it illuminated every street and alley like a great flash of lightning had touched down on the cloudless, arid night.

Baxter found Master Lothan on the ground clutching at his chest. He clearly had been wounded and breathed in tired sighs.

"Master!" Baxter shouted.

Lothan looked up with disbelieving shock as Baxter ran and crouched to his side.

"Why and how?" Lothan asked. "Baxter?"

"You're hurt, Master," Baxter said. He saw the stain building on the dark robe. Its reserved, simple brown color couldn't hide the substance pouring up from underneath or the hole that caused the Master's lifeforce to be draining out.

Derek mounted the stairs next. Lothan reached for a book at his side and held it up.

"I'm with him!" Derek exclaimed, holding his hands up. Lothan opened the book sternly and with force, and the pages settled into place. He groaned and lowered the book as he forced himself up against the wall again.

"What happened?" Baxter asked. "Who are they? *What* are they? I know I shouldn't be here, but now that I am, what can I do? The door is gone. Can we bar them from above somehow?"

"You're too curious," Lothan grumbled. He shut the book with one hand and did his best to punish his apprentice's unchecked want for knowledge by using the book's soft spine to tap the boy on the head— lightly in his weakened state. "And yet, you rarely learn from me." He smiled and looked at Baxter with unabashed pride. "But then, I rarely learn from myself either. Heh...." His sly laughter turned into short coughs and then painful groans.

Derek came over and started looking around. The contents of the top room were scarce compared to the stores below. It was a place of ritualistic study, with a single pedestal at chest-height in the center of the room at the center of a complex cosmic spiro-graphic pattern on the floor. Derek took down a book at random and brought it over.

"Can I tear this up?" he asked. "I just thought to do it, but these all seem kind of important."

"For what?!" Baxter exclaimed.

"For a bandage," Derek replied, tilting his head down at Lothan.

"Oh, no," Lothan said. "My life's not worth as much as any one of these. You…you put that back, thank you."

"What about the books below us?" Derek followed up.

"Don't talk about destroying books in front of the Master Archivist!" Baxter snapped. Lothan coughed again, bringing both young men back to the issue of his immediate suffering.

"Listen to me, Baxter," Lothan began. "I am Learned. I have experienced much. This isn't the first time I've been wounded to bleed. That should not be your worry. But now, you have trapped yourself in with me as my enemies no doubt have swarmed below."

"Enemies?" Baxter asked.

Lothan tried to reach behind himself to a book, huge and bound with metal and tough, armor-thick leather. Baxter saw it and reached to get it. He had to drag it into view, it was so heavy. He lifted it up and propped it on his bent knee. Lothan put his hand on top and tapped his fingers to it.

"*Daemondimonium*," he said. "*An Account of the Land of Many Daemons.* That is its full title, and that is its true purpose."

"This is…?" Baxter asked in a hushed breath. His eyes turned fully to the cover of the book. In its center was an emblem, polished and preserved, of an odd shape, mostly circular with two symmetrical divots into it that warped the outer edges to elongate. The first image it evoked in his mind was that of a ram's head with horns equally as thick as its snout glaring straight up at him in mid-charge. Behind that was a rune, a pillar with two circles circled below at its base and above at its peak. The book was familiar enough that he felt right holding it but still so foreign and new he couldn't hold back his temptation to reach for the edge to open it up.

Lothan held it shut, and his hand brought Baxter back to the present matter. "Not here," Lothan said. "This is what they want. Inside is knowledge…forbidden and dangerous."

"Who are *they*?" Derek asked. "I think this will be the third time that's been asked, if you can, sir."

"They are Shades," Lothan explained. His voice grew tired and whispery after a moment. He slid back to sit up against the wall again, and the pain returned him to a sharper tone of voice. "Shades from the Mount Abyss, from the Sea of Unlife, and the Land of Death. They are beings who exist in contrast and opposition with life itself and all that life represents. Why they have come here is unclear to me. Or, not specific enough to be certain. But I know they want the book."

"My dream," Baxter murmured. "Is this because…?"

Lothan could see the guilt in Baxter's eyes. The dreary, awful feeling building up that he was somehow to blame or that he could have stopped what happened. It warmed Lothan's heart and gave him a smile that shined through his pain. He reached his hand out to meet Baxter's. Baxter tried to keep the tome balanced on his knee with just one hand while he reached over.

Derek took the book, hefting it with ease and then holding it tight to his chest. "This thing's heavy," he said. The bluntness of his statement made Baxter crack a grin.

"Listen," Lothan began. "You cannot fret for me. I still have allies in this city that will know what I have done and what danger now abounds, but you two must flee. You cannot stay in Checcheri any longer."

"Flee to where?" Baxter asked. Derek had a mind to protest. His job, his work, and his family were there, but he could not ignore the urgency before him or the true weight the book represented in his arms.

"To Galiley," Lothan answered. "And from there, to Ishma and the Undermountains."

"But that place is in the Old World," Baxter protested. "There's no way we can charter the journey as we are. If you came, with your status, we could—"

"I am going nowhere," Lothan interrupted firmly. "I cannot defend the book here. It must be taken far away and fast. If you can, travel by night. Rest as the dawn breaks and as the sun sets. Your enemies favor darkness. Everything about them, of what they are and where they came from, is in that book." He pointed to the tome. Derek removed his arms from it as if unveiling it once again. "That is why they must claim it. The myths and legends of them are all half-formed. The truth of them—the killing truth—is there."

Baxter's breathing started to shake. With his adrenaline gone and genuine fear creeping into his heart, he couldn't think straight. He grabbed his head with his hands and shut his eyes tight.

Derek looked toward the stairs, wary that more of the strange things would come soon and that they would have little choice but to fight them in this cramped space.

Lothan saw Baxter's suffering and reached down to collect another book, which he lazily swung his way. The pages all loosened on contact and spilled half out of the binding.

"Listen," Lothan said, "everything you need to know, and you must know much, is in that book. You shall learn what to do from it, and you will accomplish something great."

"I was already trying to do that," Baxter protested. "I wanted to become the Master Archivist. To be among the Learned."

"Boy," Lothan said, his voice finally dropping down to a tone he could only hold with the last of his waking energy, "you become Learned by learning. First with the eyes, then with the mind and heart and soul. I could tell you everything I know from now on, but then, would you have really learned anything at all that way?" He smiled and half-winked.

Baxter took in the words of his Master, always teaching and always positive, with grave seriousness.

"I would," Derek said. "If you told me, that is, I'd learn it. If you think you'll live long enough to explain it."

"Derek," Baxter warned as he rose to his feet.

"I'm sorry," Derek replied. "I say dumb things when I'm feeling anxious. I've never hung around with a dying man before. I'm sorry. I don't mean to—"

"You're right."

Baxter spoke with such honesty and level-headedness that Derek had to do a doubletake to Lothan, who was still conscious and looking proud at his apprentice. "Well, yeah," Derek agreed, "but…I didn't mean to say—"

"We don't have time," Baxter affirmed. He almost turned to look on Lothan once more but stopped himself and faced the stairs. "They'll be coming up again. If we take the book away, they'll leave this place as well."

"Sure," Derek said. "But if they're coming up while we're going down, there's only one way it'll end up for us."

"Not if you have the book," Baxter told him.

"Mate, I can't even read the job postings," he said. "That's why I joined the union."

Baxter moved up his arms, mimicking the same position Derek used to hold the book, fingers tight around its solid edges with the spine down. Then he lifted his arms and lowered them as if placing the book before him. "Is it heavier than a stone block?"

"Not at all," Derek answered. "As a brick or two."

"Can you swing it?" Baxter asked.

Derek finally got what he was saying and looked down at the book in his hands as if it were a weapon.

"Oh, you can't do that while stoney-ing," he said, still awkwardly chuckling. "You hammer-drop a stone like that, and you'll be kicked into the gaol before break."

"We already broke one rule," Baxter reminded him. He shrugged his head to the side. "Let's keep going and see what's under all the rubble afterward."

Derek nodded and took the lead. He glanced down the stairwell that led to the floor below and then flattened into the floor itself before more stairs continued down. "That's a lot of stairs," he said before appraising Baxter. "You should be stronger than you are!" He started down with the book held out in front of him. He treated it like a stone and carried it tightly while minding the corners. Baxter hesitated before he followed. In his mind, it was a strategic move not to get in his way should an enemy somehow surprise Derek so he could assist from behind. But his heart knew he had hesitated because his Master had reclined against the wall and gave no more words to send him off. He went silent, and Baxter left.

Derek charged down the stairs, stomping down like he was chasing a runaway rockslide of precious building tools. From around the perpetually rounding corner, he saw a creature ascending, human-shaped but dog-like in posture. It was covered in black, no flesh of any kind exposed, all of it either skin-tight cloth or rugged leathery straps connecting randomly like a poor man's prison binding. He jumped up at him with long, clawed fingers.

Derek gritted his teeth, roared mightily, and swung the book spine-down onto its head. The creature spiked onto the floor with a crash as the book bounced off. The assailant's body jerked around the fulcrum of its neck and it did not move again. Derek lifted the book back up over his head and looked at the bottom. The spine was unmolested. The studs of metal in the clasps along its edge made it sturdy.

"This is a good book!" he exclaimed.

Baxter charged down after him. Derek advanced, book overhead, ready to smash, while Baxter observed the still body of the Shade. Its body was diminished where the light of the lantern in the room touched it. It slowly dissolved, like chalk in water, and the stray remnants off its body floated away and dissolved into the shadows, unseen and immaterial. He ran after Derek to the base of the tower, ever closer to an ominous blue glow that seeped into the tower from below like a cloud of smoke. Their enemies awaited there, and by Derek's mighty arms, they'd get their book, smashed right against their eyes with the force of a falling mason stone.

9

Derek hit the ground floor, book up and ready to swing. The blue light from the Archive flooded in and surrounded him. It was glaring to his eyes, unnatural light he'd never experienced before. He held the book up in front of his face to block just a bit of it while leaving some space to see ahead. The doorway was enveloped in a hazy aura he couldn't see past, like a gate of light leading from a pitch-dark cabin to the blinding noon sun outside.

"Baxter?" Derek called. Baxter appeared behind him, tired from the fast descent but prodded forward, buzzing from the flight of excitement that drove them both.

"Is the book all right?" Baxter asked.

Derek lifted it up a bit to show it off.

"Not a dent," he said. "Hard as stone!"

"Harder than their heads," Baxter added. "Whatever they are."

"Shades, 'innit?" Derek asked.

"That's not a helpful description," Baxter replied.

"Your…," Derek started, then nodded up toward the stairs. "Your guy up there said as much."

"Shades refer to a host of different mythical creatures," Baxter explained. He pressed himself against the wall and edged himself toward the doorway to peer through stealthily. He saw through the glaring wall and searched the blue light for signs of movement. There were certainly shadows on the floor level—shades of the bookcases and the reading tables and the disorderly chairs that had been scattered around the area. Nothing standing or moving, though.

"I'll watch your back," Baxter offered.

"Okay," Derek replied. "Just say so, and I'll swing full around."

"Well, all right. Then I'll stand away," Baxter said. He waved Derek on and then followed. Derek stepped out bravely, chest out and arms flexed, holding the tome of destiny in his grip like a heavy slab on its way to a lock-stone wall. It was less blindingly bright but more obnoxiously vibrant on the ground floor. The sconces and torch holders on the walls were all lit with the mysterious blue flames. The room felt cold despite its brightness.

"Can't even have normal fires," Derek commented. "Just gotta be different for no sake."

"Real light hurts them," Baxter said as he crept up behind him. "If we can find and light a torch or lantern, we can keep them at bay and flee."

"Flee where?" Derek asked. "Just hoof it and run five days out to Galiley? Even on a trade horse, it takes two nights to travel the roads."

"Then we'll…," Baxter began, trying to form a plan on the spot with no solid guidance, no experience with the Guilds or connections therein, and no assets or favors to claim from anyone in the know who could help him. He was at a total loss as to what to do. Running on foot through the night would be deadly, even without their supernatural pursuers.

"Hey," Derek whispered. He turned to Baxter and nodded to the side. There was a figure approaching, silhouetted by the blue lights behind it. It walked upright in tired, stomping steps. The sounds of strained groaning in a young woman's voice were heard. Baxter came forward, hiding behind Derek like he was a wall while peering around him to observe what was coming.

"It's Marley," Baxter said. The girl, disheveled and shaking, trudged forward with her arms limply drifting at her sides. "She's the night-watch Librarian's aid."

"She's that girl you talked about?" Derek asked. "The cute one?"

"I never—," Baxter stopped himself. "Something's wrong with her."

"Well, she's alive," Derek noted. "We ought to get her out with us."

"Wait," Baxter whispered. "She's the servant of a nobleman. We could pry a favor if we save her."

"I don't like nobleman's favors," Derek said, reacting pensively. "They always rope you into some long, awful ordeal for their benefit only."

"We'll be out of the Empire in a few days if all goes well," Baxter reassured him. "We have no debts to be gained."

Derek sighed and rolled his eyes. He wasn't having that notion. He'd worked on the ground for nobles, heard their dictations, and followed their strange, circuitous orders. Even if the nobleman happened to be a pleasant person who valued their servants and had an endearing heart of philanthropic good, they would still need a profit to come out of any favor asked of them.

Derek stepped forward with the book down. "Evening, miss!" he charmingly said.

Marley's eyes were white, her skin gray, her veins black, and her temperance aggressive. She growled and reached forward, arms flayed out toward the book as if desperate to grasp it. Her white eyes started burning blue as she grappled with the edges. Derek felt her tugging at it and was surprised at her strength. She wasn't just shifting its balance; she was forcing it away from him. So, he pushed back and smacked her in the face. She barked out and fell over.

"I thought you said this girl was cute!" Derek said, looking down at the twisted girl. Baxter looked irked by the comment. Suddenly, the lights started to go out one at a time. Slowly, the room behind them darkened. The shadows in the absence of light seemed murky and deep, like a wall of water moving in behind them.

"Run to the entrance," Baxter hissed. He and Derek both hopped over and past Marley's writhing body on the ground as she struggled to find equilibrium between the pain and her unnatural disposition. She reached after them until the darkness passed over her as well. Derek led the way and clattered against the furniture, issuing a quick half-curse words with each impact. He could see the wide doors at the front of the cathedral, just barely lit from the moon outside.

Then it went dark as if their eyes were forced shut. Derek couldn't even see the book in his hands, and Baxter couldn't see Derek in front of him. They ran into each other, and Baxter immediately searched for Derek's belt to hold onto. "Right, so," Derek began, "just shout if you need me."

"If they let me," Baxter muttered. He had nothing on his person that could help, not a spare candle for changing out reading lights or a lantern at his side for touring the city at night. He had his wits, which were muted by the darkness, and the book that contained some dark destiny that Derek kept in his mighty grip. They had no way of navigating and nowhere to go.

Then, ahead of them, standing in front of the cathedral door was a figure. Even within the darkness, he stood out as something darker still. The absence of light and his ever-darkening form and armor made them feel as though they had entered a deep void where the sun couldn't reach. Derek held his breath, and Baxter failed to gasp in time. He couldn't breathe at all. They were submerged in darkness, and it pressed on them like an ocean of water.

The Shade Lord stepped forward, bearing blue flames that lit nothing around them. His clawed crown and sharp-edged armor shimmered like the moonlight off of water. He came just out of reach of Derek and stood firm. His breath was strange and hollow. It was like he did not exhale or inhale of his own accord but allowed the wind to pass through a cavity in his throat instead, and his body was dead still. His eyes were focused on the book, the *Daemondimonium.*

"What? You want it?" Derek asked aggressively. "I-I'll give it to you, then…." His nerves betrayed his demeanor.

The Shade Lord started raising its arm to reach for it. It hissed out a hideous sound that somehow formed a word.

"Walker…."

The voice rattled like blocks of stone grinding together. It was a familiar, uncomfortable, and awful sound that froze Derek on the spot. His instincts as a mason, as a laborer, and as a human being were all tested out as the hand came at him, a single oily shimmer in a solid black sea. Baxter moved in front and put his hand over the book to block it, as best and as feebly as he could. His sudden presence shook Derek out of his stillness.

"Get back," Baxter quietly demanded. The darkness made him quieter as if the very air was too heavy to let him lift his whole voice up his throat. "Get back, or I'll…I'll read it!"

There was no response. The reaching hand just stopped in place. Then it changed its position. The fingers curled in, all but one, the index finger pointing forward like a dagger slowly inching toward Baxter's face. He was stunned with fear and clenched his eyes tight.

Bright light suddenly blasted away the darkness. The doors flew open, and a sunlike power banished the shadows away in the entry lobby. The Shade Lord Victus stood, still reaching, but turned and was unsettled by the sudden appearance. First came one glaring, brilliantly orange light, then another, like two suns swinging in the air before all three. Derek and Baxter shielded their eyes with their hands while the Shade Lord staggered away from them, stumbling further and further back until it nearly fell over.

Victus hung, one foot still planted and leg bent, just above the floor. He fell but did not land. With just one leg he stayed aloft and hung above the stone floor like he was reclining on an unseen band of string. His armor slowly started to regain its blue glow, bit by bit, until it swelled up and reached his face.

"Come on!" a voice called out, a lady working against time and reason. "Get out now!"

Derek and Baxter, uncertain of the consequences if they ignored the woman's request, took her side and ran toward the lights. As they got closer, their eyes adjusted from the glaring flashes, and they saw a young woman about their age, holding up two lanterns that were blazing at full brightness above her head. They ran past her and out of the cathedral. Once they were past her, she looked over the scene.

She could see the fog of darkness roiling behind the Shade Lord. Victus rose again to both feet and glowered at her. She started retreating, her legs twitching and half-jumping away. She looked around on reflex and found a standing hanger full of dusty old robes near the wall. She hung one lantern off the nearest branch and took the other with her out of the cathedral and into the street. Victus took a step forward, then put one foot directly in the path of the brightest light. He stopped there, and the mass of bodies that mingled and mixed gaseously behind him quivered in his immediate shadow.

Outside, the boys collected their breath for the first time, inhaling real night air, and looked themselves over. Derek still had the book, and Baxter still had his eyes. The girl, Eidel, held her lantern over them and checked the streets for any onlookers. There were people in the distance—most likely guards who weren't paying them any attention—and others down the street braving the night to attend to poorly lit chores or illicit routines. The main street all the way down to the ports and trading posts was alight with the late-night merriment from each and every inn and tavern along the way.

"I'm never closing my eyes again," Derek decided. "That was so dark I couldn't breathe."

"It's real," Baxter said. "The myths and the Abyss…. It's all—"

"Are you two going to have a breakdown right now?" Eidel asked. Baxter turned to her, and they both shared an awkward, sudden second meeting. The unfortunate inconvenience flashed through both their minds, but Eidel was the only one composed enough to comment on it. She looked down at his shoes and pursed her lips. "You're not going to trip again while walking, are you?"

"No," Baxter said. He straightened out his overcoat and tried to square himself up proudly. "No, but we will be running. Thank you for your help, and as for why you did it, I won't ask."

"You should," she said. "I saw you enter the cathedral, and those monstrous things followed you in through that dark, abysmal alley."

Baxter's heart sank, abruptly consumed by guilt. He had been willingly denying it for a time, but hearing it confirmed sent him into a spiral of despair. Fortunately, Derek caught him with a shoulder grab and braced him to stand up fully with the heavy book hoisted under his arm.

"If we're going to be passing off blame for anything," Derek said, "we shouldn't blame each other. Some stones roll. We can blame the carver or the lifter or the mason or the foreman, but if it hits a man, we mourn. If it hits the floor, we'd best laugh it off, yeah?"

"What?" Eidel asked in a huff.

"Yeah, I get it," Baxter said. He sighed and reorganized his thoughts in the brief moment in which Eidel threw a curled-lipped expression of befuddlement at Derek, who just smiled and nodded. "We need to get out of the city."

"Oh, do you?" Eidel asked.

"Yes," Baxter began. He spoke rapidly, but very clearly, and somewhat quietly, which caused Eidel to move in closer, which made Baxter even more nervous. "Because those Shades are after the book, the *Daemondimonium*, which holds secrets that they need to keep sealed for their own benefit. The destination that the book must travel to is the Undermountains of Ishma in the Old World, which is an entire length of no less than three countries away outside of this one, and the closest place to begin that journey is Galiley, which is where Master Lothan of the Archive, my Master, has instructed me to go."

"I was there for that," Derek said. "It all checks out."

Eidel looked between them. Baxter's rushed, impatient prattle and Derek's calm, apparently accepting demeanor were too much for her tired mind. She was just trying to stalk her father's mysterious customers to prove they were breaking Guild statutes so she could cancel their contract and claim a reward for turning them in. She wasn't prepared to involve herself with a conspiracy or a parade through foreign lands.

"All right," she began. "You said that book has…secrets?"

"Many," Baxter replied. Derek held the book up and nodded, giving his own approval, for whatever it was worth.

"And those Shades," she continued, pausing just to digest the fact that she had said the word with the same gravity that Baxter had, "they want it because it will help them?"

"It may empower them," Baxter explained. "I'm…not sure precisely what it may do."

"Lothan said," Derek added, "everything to know about them is in the book, yeah? So, maybe a way to defeat them. Since they're…what was it? Unlife and anti-living. And such."

"Right," Baxter said, facing his friend. "The myths of Shades are all…murky at best from what I know. But we do know for certain they can't tolerate light."

"Come with me," Eidel beckoned. The boys turned to her and saw her more determined than before. The gears were turning in her head while they were talking, and she seemed to have a much better reason for helping them than before. "I can get you to Galiley."

10

Eidel guided her two miscreant, mysterious allies through the streets in the quiet doldrums of the night. The taverns were noisy, but outside, there was peace. The sound of drunkards laughing, shouting, or singing songs changed from one establishment to the next. The working class of laborers and merchants all mingled together, enjoying the fruits of their labors fermented and served with foam into mugs and pints to close out their day so they could awaken in the morning with a headache and a scowl.

It seemed to be pure luck that she managed to find the two in time. Her pursuit of her father's strange and illicit benefactors was, initially, out of subterfuge-ish curiosity. If they were brought into the city for illegal means, she planned to reliably feign innocence on the charges of aid and claim she had thought the cart was only stocked with supplies when in fact the benefactors must have hidden inside of it. That was the truth, although the participation of her father would be greatly underrepresented. He was knowing and seemed willing to assist, though as for the reason why she had no idea. Even if it was for money, he wasn't foolish enough to entertain such strange and demented actions.

"So," Baxter said, "you're a Night Porter?"

"No," she replied. "I'm a regular Porter." She didn't want small talk to mix in with her dire duty. She had her own concerns and reasons for helping them. If they had the secrets of the Shades in their hands, she would use them. She remembered seeing her father taken by the Shade Lord's hand and the strange ritual that commenced. It was still in him, a strange darkness. He acted normal, but a deeper shadow covered him than normal.

"Porters have good horses," Derek said. "We might get to Galiley sooner than we thought!"

"I'm not sure how to make all of this work," Baxter admitted. "I mean, as payment."

"You'll pay me when we get there," she said. "With that book."

"The book is not for trade," Baxter said forcefully. Derek held it close in response, as its keeper.

"I mean for you to read it," Eidel corrected. "As I cannot."

"Oh," Baxter said. "You-you wish for me to pay you with my labor, is it?"

"Reading is not a labor," Eidel argued. "It is a skill and a trade."

"If you'd read some of the things I have," Baxter said, "you may disagree. The small-printed words or indecipherable scribbles of hand-printing can strain the eyes and the mind as well."

"Do eyes have muscles?" Derek asked.

"Yes," Baxter answered. "Little thin ones, mostly around them." He circled the shape of his eye. Derek nodded in understanding.

Eidel stopped just before the last turn of the street that led to her home. The lower Merchant Quarter was the place of all the first stops and carriage rides. It was a horse road firstly and not maintained or kept clean for daily peasantry. "If there are secrets of these creatures in there," she said, "then I want to know them. All of them. To stop them."

"That's a strange vindication you have," Baxter said. "Why take such a personal aim against these beings? We're the ones who were nearly harmed."

"Mostly unharmed," Derek corrected fruitlessly.

"It's my father," she said. She began her grand lie there with them. "He was tricked. He took in a carriage the night before this, and those creeping figures emerged from it. They threatened him, and their leader did something strange that captivated my father to follow their orders. Please, you must help my father. Release him from their curse."

"Oh," Baxter said. He looked to the book. Already it was calling to him to offer aid, and he could feel its weight in his arms, too much to bear or hold aloft. He saw Derek comfortably holding it to his side and caught a smile from his hulking friend. He was carrying it so easily, the burden of its weight and importance and the power it had to help or hurt others. "Well…I know better than to negotiate with a Porter on the walk. I'll, uh, I'll try."

"Good," Eidel said. "And once he's well, we can be on our way."

"How long will that take, do you reckon?" Derek asked. His question halted Eidel in mid-step before Baxter could think it through properly.

"It's a massive book," Baxter said. "Starting from the beginning, it may take a full day to read. It may take longer. It might be in a different language. We haven't even opened it yet to see."

"Will that be a problem?" Derek asked.

"I only know a few languages," Baxter admitted.

"That's a few more than I do!" Derek said.

"Boys!" Eidel hissed. She settled her voice back down and nodded for them to follow. "Inside. In the light, perhaps?"

"Oh, right," Baxter recalled. "The demons." They rushed over to Eidel and followed her in a steady, marching walk through the narrow side streets to her house. Baxter was immediately suspicious when she entered. It was a lesser home, unattractive and off the main path with only one door for the garage and only room for one cart at a time—a small, lesser house among Porters.

Inside was little better. The house portion reminded Baxter of his own home, although less rowdy. It was cramped and stacked with unused things that couldn't be removed, broken chairs and crates that belonged in a storehouse somewhere else, with stairs to a second story where all the beds he didn't see were likely hiding. Eidel set her lantern on the nearest table in the center of the room and gently crept over to fetch a stable chair.

"Eidel?" a man called out from above. Footsteps came rushing down the stairs. Baxter and Derek nearly dove out the door, but Eidel looked their way and waved them in. Torn between the fear of the owner's judgment over their appearance in this home and defying the stern girl's command, they stayed put, and Derek slowly pushed the door shut. Mr. Laun came down, restless and frazzled. Dark circles were under his eyes that weren't there before as if shadows had gathered just beneath his vision. He looked changed and tired, years older than he had been yesterday.

"Where did you go this late?" he asked, with sincere worry in his voice. "You thought you went out unseen? With lanterns in hand, even before the twilight hours ended? Did you think I wouldn't hear the latch of my own door? And you bring back strangers?"

"Father," Eidel said, "please stop and let me explain."

"Explain what?" he asked.

"Father," she said more sternly, with an unwavering voice that silenced his quivering, uncertain candor. "Those men you ported in, they attacked the Archive. I followed them. I watched them. I saw their ill intent in action."

"Oh, no." He clutched his head and shook it gently.

"It's okay," she said. "We can surrender their payment. If we catch them, the Guild will reward us, not punish us."

"No, no," he muttered. "No, the payment, the payment isn't-it's not...." He was stuttering and panicked. His secret deal was revealed—and to his own daughter. As close as they were as father and daughter, he knew he didn't have the will to control her as he had to. "We can't return a payment we never received."

"What?" she asked. She still didn't know what risk he had taken that was worth the whole of their family name. Some money would make sense, fine goods or exotic materials to trade, exclusive rights to rate works of art, something noble and righteous or pilfered and illicit, even just a written promise or favor from another whom the Guild could seek compensation from in retaliation for abusing the trust of a kind and desperate Porter in their care. It couldn't be nothing.

"It can't be for nothing!" she snapped. She grew flustered and mimicked her father, patting the sides of her head and straining not to grab her own hair. Baxter and Derek quietly moved to sit at the table with the lantern. Derek propped the book up and lowered it gently onto the table. It slid out of his fingers and hit the table's surface with a bang.

"Shh!" Baxter hushed.

"Sorry!" Derek said with his hands up and out, a natural reflex to save his precious fingers from a fallen stone.

"Sorry," Baxter parroted back. His reaction was equally reflexive, honed from his time in the forced quiet of the Archive where even breathing too loudly was an offense worthy of ejection.

"It was for nothing," her father said. "The wares are all dust and clay, either fakes or antiques without value. Just dirt. The carriage itself is not worthless, but it's too foreign to pass. If it were seen in the streets under daylight it would be mistaken for an invader in the city. They've left us nothing."

"What about your eyes?" Eidel asked. "I saw when they emerged. I was there watching. I saw what they did. What did they do to your eyes?"

"Even that," he admitted. He was starting to tear up but held back his crying for the sake of fatherly pride. "Even that, I do not know. I see some things here and there, visions that don't seem real, made of blue fire. Markings, like sign-work. When I reach out to touch them, my hand passes through. And, in the dark, I can see very well. That's it. Their payment was in that. I cannot give up my own eyes as recompense. What good would capturing them do if I would have to surrender my eyes to the Guild as false payment?"

"Those Shades," Derek said, "must have strong eye muscles to see in the dark." He turned to Baxter for a reaction, but Baxter had none for him. Instead, he ducked his head just before Eidel heard and stomped her way over. Derek saw her coming and put his hands up to defend himself. She glared at the book and reached over to force it open. The lock would not budge.

"Open this now!" she demanded. "Open it and undo my father's curse!"

"All right, calm down," Baxter soothed. "Now, as unfortunate as this all is for you, as a Porter, I think we still have something to discuss."

"You'd take advantage of my family in our needing time?" she asked incredulously.

"You," Baxter began, "you said…. You agreed to this! You said we'd have a ride to Galiley if I helped you. We can't stay in this city while the Shades are around. We need to travel by night while they're moving and rest in the day while the sun impedes them. Right?"

"That's what Lothan said," Derek confirmed. They both nodded together.

Eidel kept glaring them down, hard, and after a moment of enduring her intense and focused glare, Baxter stood up and started working at the binding on the book to undo it.

Mr. Laun rose up as well and went over to his daughter to try and console or calm her—or simply give a fatherly presence to the youths who were gathered at his table. He looked down at the book in question and saw the symbol on the front. It was the same one earlier drawn into the air before him by Victus, now etched in shallow lines against the hardcover. His eyes started to glow blue, and all reason and rational left his mind. His skin went gray, and his veins turned black.

"Hey," Derek called, seeing the change in Mr. Laun. He got up and prepared to stand in the man's way. Eidel looked over just as her father's mind receded fully, and he lunged at the table. Derek caught him from the front and held him back. "Hey!" he shouted again. Mr. Laun growled and snapped, throwing spittle as he reached with clawing hands past Derek's thick frame to the table. Baxter watched and retreated to the other side, leaving the table between him and the man, while Eidel shrieked and ducked away to the other side of the kitchen.

"Father, stop!" Eidel shouted.

"He's stronger than he looks!" Derek called out. Baxter looked around with worry. Every darkened corner and shadow in the room seemed like a place where a Shade could burst out suddenly and make the situation worse. Then he looked at the book. The book the Shades wanted, and the blue lights from the man's eyes—just like the light from Marley's in the Archive. He dragged the book off the edge of the table and dropped it in a failed attempt to simply catch it. It slammed to the floor.

Mr. Laun started to calm down. The black veins receded, and his pallor lifted. He returned to normal after a minute, and Derek went from holding him back to holding him up.

"You good now?" Derek asked.

Mr. Laun panted and reached up to pat him on the arms.

"Eidel," he said, "you brought in a good, strong man for me to meet."

Eidel was too horrified by what she saw to react. She saw her father smiling in a smug and somewhat mocking manner as he started huffing up laughter. She laughed as well, timidly and uncertainly, until both of them were in between laughter and scared sobs. Derek lowered the man to the floor and turned around to Baxter, who was also on the floor struggling to lift the book back up.

"Lift with your legs," Derek advised.

"When he saw the book," Baxter began, his voice strained from the effort, which promptly ceased once Derek took it from him, "he lost his mind. Marley must have been the same way. This curse, whatever it is, has normal people hunting the book in the Shades' stead."

"He was normal before," Derek noted. "Didn't seem at all sinister. Kind of…pathetic, actually."

"Hmm," Baxter agreed. He turned and saw Eidel helping her father up again. Things were taking darker and darker turns, and the night was only just beginning. He made a decision and spoke with all the authority and demand he could muster, as the only one in the building with the prestige of a semi-noble profession could. "Sir, the Master Archivist has given us a mission to deliver this book away from the city with deadly urgency. The ones you ported in here, for whatever reason, are the culprits of a plot that has compromised your own safety and many others. We need to leave immediately, and as a Porter, I would like to hire you with deferred compensation to deliver us to Galiley."

Eidel looked at him while she held her fragile father up by the shoulders. She couldn't summon up her own disgust fast enough to speak out before her father said, "If that's what you need, then go." He covered his eyes and turned away. "I saw such a terrible thing, and before I knew it, I was upon you."

"It wasn't your fault, sir," Baxter said. "Once this city is safe, and once I have learned what there is to know, I will return and dispel this hold they have on you. I promise that."

"Thank you," Mr. Laun said. "Eidel…a Porter must be present on all deliveries between cities."

"Father, I…." She couldn't protest. It was rare, but when her father was of the mood and had good reasons, he could act as a proper father and a fine Porter as well.

"I think you're strong enough," he said proudly, "to take up your very first Night Porting route." He smiled at her. The corner of his cracked lips lifted up the dusty, dark hue of his whiskers. His belief in her, and his pride as a father, sank her own ambitions in an instant. She had a job to do, and as a Porter, not even the devils of another land could stop her from making her delivery.

II

The gates to Checcheri were watched over day and night by a rotation of guards who were employed by a variety of the noble houses. There was no need for a military presence in an era of peace, but there was always the threat and looming danger of contraband and illicit goods entering or exiting the city to promote crime abroad. However, the gates could not stay closed at any time, as opening them caused a great ruckus and could happen at any time when traders came. So, they stayed open, and narrow liners of wooden barricades would line the way and restrict the travelers from going through at any speed.

The guards of the southeastern gatehouse, closest to the Porter district of the Merchant Quarter, saw a cart approaching with great speed, pulled by two horses stomping out a fever with their hooves in the dead of night. The cart was long and narrow and lazily covered from end to end with a flittering tarp. The guards tried to mobilize just to see it go by as it sped past. It was moving too quickly, and the make of the cart was very strange. The edges of the wheels were spiked and the whole frame was braced with rough metal like a war-cart. The late hours were the ideal time for barricade runners to make themselves known as no one in the city's guard would care enough to chase them down.

The carriage plowed through the flimsy, spare-wood, sawhorse blockers and stormed out of the gates, leaving behind a trail of dust and straw in its wake. The make of the carriage was noted by the guards on response, and the place it came from was investigated immediately. A lone guard was dispatched to begin questioning the lesser houses among the Porter district to see who could have let such a thing happen and what excuse they might have for letting a cart go missing.

That guard walked out of the light and into a dark alley, near the Laun house, which he set his eyes on first. The carriage hall was open, and the lights were out. At best, it could have been a theft, and the Porter in charge would have to manage their insurance with the Guild for recompense. He failed to consider something worse and was quickly apprehended by an armored, metal hand. Before he even had a chance to struggle, his breath left him, becoming a cold, foggy trail in the air that seeped into the open visor of Victus's helmet. He dropped the man and drew a command in the air. The guard blankly stared and then shifted in place. Then, he turned and guarded the alley mindlessly.

A Shade emerged from the garage where the rest were swarming, climbing, and crawling all around the walls and ceiling of the darkened building. "Gone," it whispered. Victus lowed and nodded. He looked toward the house. "Asleep," the Shade said. Victus huffed.

"The book was here," he rasped. "It can only leave so quickly…." Victus swung his arm into the air, and the Shades dispersed to the roofs. He joined them, weightlessly hopping one heel-toe step at a time across the reach of homes and Merchant fronts toward the edge of the city, then toward the main gates, and finally on toward the long, rolling pastures that separated the great city from its nearest neighbor.

Far out from there, already making distance that reduced the great mounted city to a shimmering pile that rose over the horizon, Eidel directed the horses to a speedy gallop while Baxter and Derek sat hunched down under the tarp in the back as her cargo. She looked back once to admire the sight of the city from afar, one she hadn't seen since she was a child, a sight both boys beheld for the very first time with growing wistful remorse.

"Do you see them?" she called out. Baxter turned back, almost surprised by her question, and returned to staring out the back as the landscape sped away. The sight of his home—and his ambition—receding quickly into the distance drew his attention back down to the heavy book under his hand. His new goal, given but not yet gained, something important but without proper explanation, was right there with him. He turned to Derek and saw him suffering. The parting was too fast for him, and the stripping of his responsibilities—and essentially his past life—was all Baxter's doing.

"You okay?" Baxter asked.

"Ugh," Derek burped. "I can't handle this," he said. "It's too much muh-movement. I'm gonna…I didn't eat much today, but I feel like it's…."

Baxter hastily dragged the book from him and hauled it over to the other side of the carriage. "Not on the book," he warned, then pointed to the back of the cart, the edge of which Derek crawled toward just in case. His motion sickness notwithstanding, he also felt a grim premonition of their travels as they fled the city. He was leaving more than just his own ambitions behind. His first thoughts were of his work.

"They'll get on fine without me," Derek muttered for the sake of self-comfort. "They've got...." He rubbed his face down as a cold sweat broke out, a threat of sickness yet to come.

Meanwhile, Baxter pushed the book up toward the front of the long carriage and kept it under his knee so it wouldn't slide away.

"I don't see anything chasing us," Baxter announced. "No guards, and no dark entities dressed to blend in with the expansive darkness of an unlit, wilderness night."

"Don't you dare snip at me!" Eidel exclaimed. "I reserve full contractual rights to all snippiness from here on in until the job is concluded."

"Can Porters really trade in human emotions like that?" Baxter retorted.

She whipped the reins in response, and the horses replied in turn with a burst of speed.

Baxter held onto the rim of the carriage and kept his bodyweight on the top of the book. It had already proved robust enough to endure several mallet-like blows, so he trusted it to bear his weight as well.

"I mean it!" Eidel shouted over the sounds of rushing air and sprinting hooves. "First, my father falls to an illness of insanity, all because of that book that the Archivist had. If it's so damn important, why cling to it? They may just take it and leave us all alone!"

"I doubt my Master's murderers have any kind of peace on their minds," Baxter replied. Eidel didn't retort immediately, but she wanted to, and he could tell. Even raising his own loss against that of her father, who was still well and able-bodied, didn't dismiss her arrogant offense.

"We should have warned the guards in the gatehouse," she continued. "They could have spotted the Shades and fought them off."

"And it would have involved more people," Baxter countered, "and spread a wave of panic through the city, all of which would have been investigated to find out where the monsters had come from. Which would have led them where, Ms....?" Baxter paused just as Eidel reached a high point of quiet fuming. "I'm sorry. I think I missed your name. Is it Beetle?"

Eidel glared back, reached over, grabbed the top of his head and pushed him down under the tarp again. "It's Eidel!"

"Right, got it," Baxter muttered quickly. He stayed down and palmed at his head where she had grabbed him. He waited there in darkness, transparent but still oppressive shadows under the covers, and felt a mix of dreadful anxiety and physical exhaustion creeping up on him. It was past his and Derek's routine bedtimes, and they were on an ongoing flight away from danger. It seemed like a perfect time to get some rest while it was still night out, but he remembered his Master's words and advice: to sleep in the day when the Shades could not travel.

His first night outside of Checcheri was spent rocked and jostled by the constant rumbling of running horses. Derek's was spent desperately keeping himself balanced so his face was over the rear back of the carriage while the rest of his body stayed within it. The open back of the cart meant no one could sleep while they moved without being tied down first. The few empty crates and cases that were left behind from the Shades had spilled out immediately after they took off.

They rode on for what felt like hours. Baxter fought off drifting into sleep by alternating which arm to tuck under the *Daemondimonium* so the pain would keep him awake. Eidel, meanwhile, was a tireless woman with a will of steel who stayed awake, fueled by conviction and rage. She drove the horses to exhaustion until finally, hours after leaving, when Checcheri was as distant as a star in the sky, and the unlikely travelers had journeyed out into the long expanses of countryside and just outside of the covered forest trails, she gave them a break. The horses slowed to a stop and huffed loud, grumbling breaths. They were all-day walking horses; their stamina was better left to slower rides, but they were loyal.

"What happened?" Baxter asked. He poked his head up through the tarp and looked around. It was still dark out, far more than before. There weren't even the distant lights of the city to rely on. It was just them and the stars and the gray, shadow-soaked lands that surrounded them. Every dark corner and shadow under a tree were new avenues for the attackers to potentially appear out of.

"The horses need a rest," Eidel said. "Not a long one. They can walk on for another day." She turned around. Baxter could see, even under the dim moonlight and the harsh dark of the lightless country around them, a glimmer of tears in her eyes that she fought off and wiped away. "Can you hand me the feed bag from the back?"

"Sure," Baxter said. He was so immediately taken by her that the situation hadn't dawned on him fully that she was asking him to lift something heavy. It wasn't until he forced himself to drag the bag out that he realized his folly, and Derek couldn't help, since he had somehow managed to fall asleep with his head half hanging out of the back and his arm hooked around a post in the frame. It was a sleeping position only someone as strong as Derek could handle.

The bag wasn't quite as heavy as it seemed, but all of its weight sank down to one place, and it had no proper bottom Baxter could hold onto to help him anchor it in his arms. He had to haul it up by the knotted top and lugged it to the front of the cart where the horses and Eidel were waiting. It was just the two of them at that moment, both taking a quiet repose to look over their shared predicament.

"Have you been to Galiley?" Baxter asked.

"Not for a very long time," she answered. He watched her scoop up some of the ground meal from the bag and hold it up to the horse's mouth. It licked the food from her hand and munched happily. "I was born in the countryside just outside of Galiley. My father took work as a Mid-Porter out there, taking wares from the nearby storage post into the city. I went with him a few times just to see it."

"Then I suppose we'll be relying on you to be a guide as well," Baxter said. She glared at him. The hot look sent a cold chill up his spine that forced him fully awake.

"My father," she began, "took on the duty of a Porter for a small house that transferred him to Checcheri the next day. The Porter's Guild, like all Merchants, treats its workers as tools rather than people. They had no care for our family or concern over displacing us from where we had settled. They just wanted him to sway at their whim like all their other good little workers."

"Do you bear a grudge against the Guilds then," Baxter asked, taking a short pause to reconsider his line of questioning, "for forcing your father's hand?"

She sighed. His delicacy did not go unnoticed, but it wasn't effective. "He didn't go out of ignorance," she finally answered. "He knew.... He knew the consequences. He just thought we'd be better off in the end."

"Well, were you?" Baxter asked. "Or, uh, are? Are you now, still, better?"

"Have you ever fed a horse by hand?" she asked, completely denying and abandoning the subject as a mercy killing for the awkward host of bad questions.

"I haven't," Baxter admitted. "Horses intimidate me. They're very large and can kill a man with a single kick as I've read."

"Only if you scare them," she said. "And they can't kick you from the front."

"I also read," Baxter said as he took a scoop of food for the other, waiting horse, "that a horse once bit off a man's hand and ate it in front of him. Chewed it up and swallowed it, bones and all."

"What kind of person would write about such a thing?" she asked.

"It could have been real," Baxter said. "I think tonight we should all be in agreement that there are things in the world that may be unwritten but are far stranger than the myths and legends and writings of fanciful fiction."

"Right," she muttered. They drifted back into tired silence as the horses ate. Baxter felt the wet, slimy drag of the horse's tongue across his hand.

Somehow, that action reminded him of his brothers at home. He wondered if he was even missed at all or if he'd ever return.

12

Day broke over the Vincian countryside. The threat of darkness and the creatures that moved within it were gone. Across the many plains, through the wide, wild forests, and around the rolling hills and alpine mountains that tore across the Empire's lands, many people moved about their daily routines and began the process that kept the Empire alive and flourishing. Trade began before daybreak and would continue past setting suns and throughout dark nights.

The day was the finest time for traveling. Even during storms, there would be some light to guide them. The trade roads were well-established and secure with multiple checkpoints and trading posts owned and supplied by the hunting lodges and subsistence farmers who worked far away from the city-state centers. It was the noblest profession, honored even more highly than the Nobles themselves. The Merchants created value and sustained a massive economy, which supported the entire Empire, while the Nobles sat around tables in parlors inside of fancy mansions deciding how much of that money they should spend on art and finery.

The system turned many people like cogs in a great construction. Eidel was one of those cogs, as was Derek, and further removed from the metaphor was Baxter, whose role to play expanded far beyond the slight reaches of matters of the economy. He stirred from his sleep with an eerie premonition plaguing his mind. His hand reached over and clasped at an invisible quill as his wrist gesticulated across a phantom sheet of paper. His first sleep outside of the long reach of Checcheri's relative safety, and he wasn't even aware of it until after his hand stopped moving.

"Hey," Derek said. Baxter awoke with a start. He sat up and only half-opened his eyes to a blazing, bright glare that sent him right back down again. The mid-morning sun hit him in the face with more stark force than it ever could through his window. There were no walls or neighbors or mountain to stop its glaring power anymore. Not even a roof. Just a long cloth tarp acting as a waist-high roof to their backless carriage.

"You okay?" Derek asked. "Your hand was going all over."

"Ah, yeah," Baxter groaned. "I write when I wake up."

"Does everyone do that when they learn to read?" Derek asked.

"No, only me," Baxter replied, "because I want to remember what I dreamed about."

"Oh. So, what was it?" Derek asked.

Baxter sighed and shrugged. "Well, I didn't write it down. So, now, I can't remember."

Derek nodded deeply. He was sitting over the edge of the back of the cart. Baxter joined him, and he dragged the book closer so he could try and lift it up into his lap.

"You want I should try and open that?" Derek asked. Baxter just gave him a look, and he immediately relented. The book was sealed, that was true, but it wasn't bound up without intention. It was sealed for a reason; so only someone worthy of reading it could open it. The lock wasn't the kind that could just be pried away and broken off.

"Are we still moving?" Baxter asked.

"No, praise be," Derek answered with a sigh. "When we do move again, I'm sitting up front. Apparently, that helps to handle the travel-sickness better."

"Did Eidel tell you that?" Baxter asked.

"Yeah. I'm trusting her on this. She drove us a whole day's travel away. We're close to a trading port, apparently."

Baxter looked out at their surroundings. It was unrecognizable wilderness. Nothing even looked like the long, expansive horizon outside of Checcheri's walls that he could discern. The slightly familiar rolls and lulls of the land, often covered in fog from the morning and darkened with mist by night, were gone and replaced by an unimpeded, wide-open landscape of uncut woods and mountains that looked naked without the high-rising lights of cathedral glass and royal palatial homes crowning them.

"It's...quiet out here," Baxter noted.

"Yeah," Derek agreed. He sniffed the air and sighed. "We don't have any food but for that of the horses."

"Do we really not?" Baxter asked.

"We really don't," Derek replied. They took off the tarp together and bundled it up along the side. In the uncovered back, they saw a rolled-up bag of feed, good for another day of travel; an empty bucket; and the book. That was it. They had left in such a hurry—and a worthy one at that—that they failed to pack any supplies for their journey. Baxter and Derek both sighed at the realization and sat back up on the edge of the wagon.

"The human body," Baxter recited, "is capable of surviving for a week without food in ideal conditions while exerting minimal movement."

"What about unideal, and while walking the rest of the way if the horses give up?" Derek asked.

"And three days without water," Baxter added.

Derek leaned back and sighed.

"Where is Ms. Eidel now?"

"Um, off," Derek replied. "She went off to the woods to hunt up some food."

"Some berries and plants for breakfast and lunch then," Baxter said. He thought about his lost daily routine, his light breakfast leading into an absent-minded lunch and a late dinner at home after his brothers had retired for the night or before they returned home at all. The sumptuous bacon and glistening breads they ate, all dipped and soaked in sticky honey, seemed like distant dreams instead of the reviled messes they actually were. If he were lucky, they wouldn't notice his absence for a few days, at least, and if he was luckier, Master Lothan would advise them of his mission.

His head sank when he thought of his Master. He left him lying down, bleeding and motionless. It very well could have been their final parting, and he gave him no words of his own deep feelings. His appreciation, gratitude, and sadness to be gone from him had all been left unsaid. What remained was the shame of an apprentice who had left his Master early, and the likely equal shame felt by a Master who failed to pass all his teaching on in time.

"Hey," Derek said. He noticed Baxter was growing wistful and grim and patted him on the back gently to stir him out of his thoughts. He lifted the book up and set it on Baxter's lap. The weight made his friend gasp. "You want to set it on my lap instead?" Derek offered.

"Just leave it on the floor," Baxter instructed. Derek picked it up, and Baxter stood. He lifted his legs high to stretch them. The wagon's tail was just under chest-height for Baxter—about three feet off the ground—and far lower for Derek, who leaned down on his elbows to look it over. In the bright light, the book seemed grander and less menacing. The leather was fine and well-aged. The metal working within it was also expertly done and seamless. The crafting of the book was to be admired—independent of its contents.

"Right," Baxter began. "Let's open it."

"Let me know if you need my help," Derek said.

Baxter worked at the lock and found that it was knotted on the unseen underside. He felt around for a beginning or end to the cords. They felt thin and tightly wound, like the cords of a book spine. He tried to crane his head down against the flat of the wagon bed to get an angle at what he was messing with, but the latch was too narrow for light to shine on.

"At your leisure, then," Derek said. He looked up and leaned his back against the carriage. His weight, plus the weight of the book and of Baxter partially on top of the vehicle, gave just enough of a grade to the platform that the book was caught in the gravity trap and slid away from Baxter's hands. It fell and landed on its spine. Then, it opened before Baxter could even reach out powerlessly to try and stop it.

"Oops," Derek said. "I broke it."

"Did you, though?" Baxter asked. He reached down and tried to lift it. Derek helped him but only a little. With its weight dispersed and the pages having flowed toward the middle, it felt strangely lighter. Baxter set it back down and looked over the latch again. The cords were all lined up and untangled from each other. He tested the latch with a careful hand. Just lifting half of the cover was like correcting a fallen table, even without the weight of the pages as they all fell against each other.

"Well, if that's all it takes to open," Derek said, "I'm surprised it wasn't open this whole time."

"It may have been," Baxter suggested, "and you wound up locking it."

"I can't even read," Derek said defensively. "You can't expect me to know about the ways of locks on books."

Baxter smirked. His analysis drew him to conclude that he didn't understand how the locking worked, but if there was any clue as to how to open it again, the book itself would probably have the instructions. "Right. So, what is this all about?"

"Skip to the part about the Shades," Derek recommended. "That seems to be the most important matter."

"I don't even know where that would be," Baxter argued. He flipped through the first few pages. The first image both boys saw was of a man holding the very book they read, framed along the edges with text in a scrolling fashion that wrapped and curved around him. The words went from one script to another. Most of them were unknown to Baxter and put his stomach in a nervous knot. A book he couldn't read was only worth its weight in Derek's hands. Then, he saw a font he recognized and a script he could read.

"It's a name," Baxter realized.

"The whole lot of it?" Derek asked.

Baxter pointed. The script was familiar, close enough to the common language of Vincia but much older.

"Plattius Orleeus," Baxter read. "Hence did I go, to find the strangest things I could, and found them."

"What does that mean?" Derek asked. "Besides the obvious."

"It's the author," Baxter said. He pointed to the illustration, tapping around the man's face. He was garbed in Old World clothing, long and draping robes combined with tight, shoulder-strapped armor. He sported a shallow beard a shade brighter than his skin, and his eyes were drawn wider than they should have been. It was, in Baxter's view, an overall amateurish but decent illustration, most likely done by the author himself. "He must have been an explorer and wrote of all his findings here."

"Oh," Derek said. He stood up and stretched his back. "So, get to the part with how he fought off the Shades, then."

"Just hold on," Baxter said. "Books aren't meant to be rushed through and skipped along. This is the life's work of a man. A year of his journeys could have taken him ten to fully explain and elaborate upon."

"I doubt he spent a few days of those years on the drawings," Derek remarked.

The quip made Baxter chuckle slightly, but he composed himself again to continue his point.

"Everything in this book must be useful. If there was just one part meant to be forbidden, it could have been removed long ago and put somewhere safer."

"That book *is* a safe," Derek added. "Heavy as."

"There's context to consider," Baxter pressed. "There's an order in which this book was written and meant to be read. I'd like to find that order first and understand the perspective it was given. Then," his voice accelerated to the point where Derek knew he couldn't interrupt again, "we can seek the answers through interpretation. The exploits this man recorded will have an angle to their view, which will make it less ideal for pure education because it lacks a critical eye. Just like a man who's never seen a horse may make the wrong assumptions of its purpose in nature should he see one and describe it on the spot to a private audience. I must find the purpose of the writing through the text, work through that context into the narrative to find meaning, and then determine the order in which his knowledge was taken down to even find where the section on Shades might be."

"Can you read it out for me?" Derek asked. He hopped up and sat next to the book while Baxter rolled his eyes and nodded.

"I intended to," he said. "And for Eidel, if she ever comes back."

"Well, if she doesn't," Derek said as he craned his neck back to the front of the wagon, "we can still eat."

Baxter looked ahead where Derek's eyes wandered and saw only the horses. He curled his lip up in disgust.

"It's not that bad of a meat."

"We need them to take us to Galiley!" Baxter exclaimed.

"Oh, for certain," Derek said. "We need one of them, maybe."

"I'd think we'd need them both," Baxter argued.

"Hey!" Eidel shouted. She came into sight just in time to hear the tail-end of their bickering and approached with a tired scowl and a rope at her side, attached to which was a collection of hares. She raised her bounty and slapped it onto the wagon. Baxter covered the book protectively from the potential spray of dead-rabbit blood.

"Oh, good," she said. "You're finally reading. I thought you'd been bluffing about it the whole time."

"Why would I work at the Archive if I couldn't read?" Baxter asked.

She shrugged and sighed, then pointed to Derek. "Your turn."

"Can I set the fire here?" he asked as he gestured to the ground. "I don't want to miss the book reading."

"We're eating those?" Baxter asked, staring at the rabbits.

"It's meat," she answered.

Baxter turned to her and looked her over. Her Porter's apron and peasant dress looked dirtier around the knees than he remembered.

"Thank you," he said. "I wasn't aware any hunting was going on."

"Well," she began with a sigh and a forced, cordial tone, "we left in such a hurry and without any planning aside from a destination that I neglected to bring with us sufficient water or provisions from the storehouse—which was nearly barren, by the way— or any money. The only thing I was lucky to keep was my Porter sign on my dress. At the least, with this, they will see it and know that I can do business within the city, so we don't have to sneak in like criminals."

"That is good." Baxter nodded. "And I also have no money, which means…."

"It's either this or grass," Eidel finished for him. She made a smug gesture at him and patted the page of the book. "Or you could eat the paper."

"This paper is probably older than this country," Baxter said in offense.

She unlatched a rabbit from the cluster and took a knife out of her boot.

"It's probably rotten then," she said. She began skinning the rabbit right on the road while Derek hauled an armful of sticks into a ditch just off to the side. Baxter sighed and shut the book, making sure the latch did not connect and lock itself again. The reading could wait.

13

After the meal, the cleanup, and the sleepless night in full retreat, Eidel covered the carriage with the tarp and went to sleep under the relative darkness. She had the most work to do during the night, guiding them on with the Night Porter horses through long roads, through the woods, over the hills, and on toward Galiley. In that time, Derek also tried to rest on his own on the ground, something he was accustomed to on odd jobs when there were too many workers and not enough to lift.

And Baxter finally got his chance to read. The *Daemondimonium* was open before him. He finally broke past the first illustration and entered into the depths of its knowledge one deep-read at a time. As part of his preferred means of reading it out, he always had to find the voice of the writer somewhere in his head the way they must have written it. This allowed him to interpret one critically important thing about each and every text ever written: the emotion that went into it. He wanted to hear the elation of discovery, the dread of conflict, the victory after war, the scorn of lost love; all the emotions of the author were important to listen to while he read. It gave each book life beyond its intended purpose, and in that life, it gained new meanings.

The voice he found in the content was laid out bare before him. In the foreword, the author Plattius Orleeus explained his intention quite plainly in a way that even Baxter's highly active and imaginative mind couldn't make any more exciting. Baxter read: "I have compiled, herein, the full extent of the most fascinating sights and places, which I saw and traveled to in my expedition to find the Golden Mountain Root spoken of by the mad-eyed prophet whom I met behind a bar. From that impotent moment, my journey into the lost lands of Ishma begun, all on a drunken whim of boredom."

"Oh," Baxter said with a curl of disappointment to his mouth.

"Oh, what?" Derek asked, groggily. He was in and out of resting, only partially relaxed, knowing that he couldn't fight off the midday sun enough to fall fully asleep.

"This author was, uh…," Baxter struggled to find the most effectively constructive way to explain his feelings. "He was kind of a git, I think."

"Even gits can write books?" Derek asked in wonderment.

"Everyone has a story to tell," Baxter said, as though he had rehearsed the line many times. "And, unfortunately, they usually only have their own voice to tell it."

"Let me know if he talks about labor," Derek said. "I can give a better voice to that."

"I'll let you know if he complains about how heavy his book was," Baxter retorted. He continued reading past the foreword, which was also a post-script addendum, and went into the introduction. It explained in greater detail the mad-eyed prophet, a local elderly drunkard in his hometown of Ganoush who ranted and rambled at all times of the day about strange monsters and ancient demonic powers from other worlds. He also spoke of worlds within the world, hidden deep underground. Worlds of fire, sunless seas of darkness, a great sky beneath a mountain where the sun slept each night. Myths.

Plattius Orleeus revealed himself through the text to be an explorer, a man from the place they knew as the modern High World of Vincia. Back then, it was a collection of scattered, stalemate imperial powers all vying for territory during the Age of Conquest. He left his homeland in search of peace in the Old World countries to the east and south until he settled into Ganoush for a while. Then, after much boredom and doldrums, using his talents of study and reading to teach others his country's language, he took on the urge of traveling to Ishma, a land so ancient and distant that even the Old World cultures considered it old.

He packed his things and left the next day with a carrying case full of paper on his back. He forewent most ordinary supplies in favor of just water and a small handful of food staples to keep him going for the first long stretch of travel outside of the known territories. The first major section of the book dealt exclusively with the lands he traveled through. The port town of Lafell, the rich city in the steppes called

Shish, and the ancient pasture lands of Toppa. That was the last kind-hearted land he went through, and it was where his composition started.

Baxter read, "In the last night of my stay in Toppa, I'd heard mention of a daemon that preys upon the goats they herd in the craggy, rocky pasture lands they hold dear. It was very goatlike in form with great tall horns sticking out of its furry head and a long, matted beard under its chin. However, it had the stature and shape of a man, some ten feet tall. Its body was scaled like a lizard's hide, and it had great talon claws for its hands and thick, trunk-like, clubbed feet with toes all compacted down to the ground, almost like a fleshy hoof.

"I tried to illustrate such a monster with their guidance, and this is the closest approximation I could render before my light burnt out." Depicted on the side of the page was one such illustration; however, in what seemed a kind of tradition in this author's drawings, the eyes were too wide, too spaced out, and sort of left the creature's head on either side. The rest was passable, but the eyes were always just a bit too big and malformed. And of course, the pupils were wrong. They split into a cross-formation, not the vertical shape of a standard goat's, daemonic or otherwise.

"Additions were added after the fact when the daemon was captured later that night," Baxter read, with some shock. There was no establishment or any setup to reveal that such a thing was possible in the book, before or after. "The shepherds invited me to see the beast in its dying breaths. They'd speared it through many times with long throwing spears with jagged ends to stay stuck once the flesh was pierced—quite brutally—and ropes on the end to tie the spears to posts in the ground. It was on its back and wheezing breath with a long, three-forked tongue sticking out. I saw its eyes, and it had cross-shaped pupils that seemed to twist and contract as it observed me. They may have been X-shaped. The point is, they could rotate. I know not why."

"Well," Baxter sighed, "I have a miserable feeling in the pit of my stomach that this might not be the bastion of aid and knowledge it was once foretold to be."

"You sayin'," Derek groggily spoke, "your guy might've lied to get it off his own hands?"

"I don't doubt this is important," Baxter said with a tinge of defeat in his voice. "Just, perhaps, to someone else."

"He's got you go-fing," Derek said. Baxter looked at him curiously, and despite his eyes being half-closed, Derek could feel the confusion bearing down on him. "Go fetch, go off and get something for him, or in this case, deliver it. Go-fing."

"Is that like stoning?"

"Stoney-ing," Derek corrected. "Stoning is-is you don't want to do that to a person. That's throwing stones at a person to kill 'em."

"So, you call hauling stones something different to avoid that stigma," Baxter realized.

"Yeah," Derek curtly concluded. "You can just skip ahead to the back, right? To the part with the Shades, wherever that is."

"I'd like not to," Baxter said, but the confidence in his voice wavered. "Well, sure. If he won't respect his own writings, then why should I?"

"There it is," Derek said. He sat up with what was left of his strength and looked himself over. They weren't in the shade; he had been slumbering lightly in the sun, and his body was starting to tan. He started crawling over to the carriage to position himself underneath it for shade, right next to where Baxter was reading.

Baxter lifted and perused each page one by one, eyes scanning many strange, oddly off illustrations of fantastical creatures and strange, humanoid anomalies.

"Now, I'm regretting this," Baxter sighed. "He made so many intriguing entries."

"Shaaaade," Derek groaned. Baxter looked down and wasn't sure if he was celebrating his return to the cool dark or making a pitiful demand for direct information.

"It's a big book," Baxter reminded his friend. "Give me a minute to find it."

"Just start at the back," Derek suggested, "and go in reverse. Shades had to be the last thing he wrote about, right?"

"No, no," Baxter said. "And see? This is precisely why I wanted to read it in its intended order. He mentioned, in the beginning, he was looking for a Golden Mountain Root. So, if there is a conclusion to his journey, it would be related to that. There could be dozens of pages detailing that journey, the journey back, his life afterward or in the interim, all sorts of things before his meeting with the Shades."

"Why are we troubled over this lad?" Derek asked. "He's been dead for thousands of years already. Why can't he just leave the world in peace?"

"We're not inconvenienced by this," Baxter protested. "It's just…there's simply a lot. You can't build a cathedral in a day, nor can you fully read a tome such as this in that timeframe."

"Meh," Derek groaned. He obviously could not easily shake off his need for sleep. Baxter also felt the drag in his legs and arms as tiredness overwhelmed him, but he wanted to make progress. Research was a long game to play. An entire book could have its meaning and importance changed by a single paragraph that changed the syntax of all the knowledge before and after it. Likewise, all the minor incidents he had passed by in the diary filled with strange drawings and their meanings could hold necessary secrets for learning the final piece of their more-personal puzzle.

Finally, he reached a page that caught his eye immediately. A simple illustration of shadows of men that were drawn against a fixed perspective of ground with what looked like a goat for scale. They were all black and drawn with smudged ink. They had no features, just shadows with depth that stood up from the ground. Shades.

Baxter read to himself, "On the outskirts of an ancient, abandoned town far into the Ishma province, I found myself surrounded by strange people who had no features and were covered with shadow. They walked and made their own way only at night and happened on my camp on the hill overlooking the valley village. They stayed out of the reach of my fire and would not approach it even as I beckoned them. I tried to share a piece of my frog steak with them, but they did not accept. I tried to communicate over and over, to no response. I felt a bit uneasy, but strangely not unsafe. I went into the dark with them, away from my fire, and went closer to them.

"To say about them, these shadowy men, they are very cold to the touch and wet. Clammy is a fair word. It occurred to me then that they were not simply darkened by the lack of light. There was a presence covering them completely, a physical darkness that dripped over them, not unlike wet ink, but more persistent, and it came off them as a light, lingering fog that circled them. They were amicable to my approach, at least, and gave me no troubles. I saw them retreat into the village after some time, perhaps once they assessed I was a mere passing stranger who had no qualms against them, and I did not see them again.

"Come morning, I went to investigate to see if perhaps the Shades were creatures of the night like the Wastemare before them or what they did in the hours where the sun was the brightest. I checked the first house that I came upon, one I was sure the Shades retreated into after they left my camp but saw nothing inside. I tried to keep the door from opening fully, knowing that they hated the light. Inside the home was just one room, small, hardly enough space even for a bed. The people of Ishma were so far ancient they had no concept of property or the need to accrue greater means. Their simplicity was striking.

"The only thing odd or off-putting was a deep hole dug into the corner beneath a window where no light could reach. I investigated and saw a movement in the dark. I tried to offer more of the remains of my late-night meal into it, and the food seemed to disappear. I tried to communicate once more with the door closed, the darkest that I could make the hovel in the middle of the day. These Shades were a rare creature I'd found, were not hostile, were human-shaped, and seemed to act in concert with one another. I could not fashion them to be monsters in my mind.

"Then I saw the Shade emerge. It spilled out at first like a lifting, heavy smoke, then reformed like water across the ground in a splash. The darker it was, the looser its form. I stood as it stood, and in the low light blocked out by the shuttered window and the quick-fitted door to the hovel home, it stood fully solid, skin all black, darker than any man's skin could be. Still, its face lacked features. I saw the contours of a face underneath like it was bound back by opaque silk. He, or she, or it had the appearance of a dark night's sky, untouched by starlight, haunted by the cover of clouds that blocked out the moon.

"It spoke to me in a harsh, whispering voice, words I could not understand. Then, it extended its hand forward and pointed at my head. I, in an attempt to find communication, reached likewise and touched my finger to its. It felt not cold nor warm. There was an absence of feeling. It was like pressing against my own finger. I could not feel any heat, only force being pushed back. Then it brushed my finger aside and stepped forward, pointing to my face, and touched my forehead. I saw flashes of dark blue light that filled my eyes and blinded me briefly. When I recovered, I saw the Shade make a motion with its hands, and as it did, a trail of blue was carved into the air. I've drawn it here. I somehow understood what it was without knowing. The knowledge was unlocked within me like a childhood memory I'd always had.

"And so, from there, I departed toward the Undermountains to find the homeland of these Shades, spurred on by invitation offered by the exchange of favors for my good deed done without thought."

Baxter looked up and realized he'd read it all, out loud, to himself. So, he closed his mouth and read with his eyes and his heart with his Master's words encouraging him.

14

When twilight finally came, Eidel rose from under the tarp fully rested and prepared to move out. She looked back to check on her cargo: the two strangers she was forced to share a meal and stay overnight with after a harrowing night of escape. She saw Derek stretching and moving around while Baxter rested on the far edge of the carriage with the mighty tome opened underneath his sleeping head. She sighed and stomped her feet on the wagon bed to startle him awake, and it worked.

"It's time," Eidel called out. "Hop up and get ready to depart. Secure everything down."

"Yessir," Derek called back. "Uh, Miss," he corrected. Eidel waved her hand away from his comment and looked down at Baxter. He slowly sat back up and looked at the book first to check on its health relative to his face, then stood up shakily on awkward, unrested legs.

"Did you find anything?" she asked. Baxter rubbed his eyes and squinted at her. His sleep hadn't been deep enough to give him the rest he needed, and his mind was lagging a few moments behind his body as a result.

"Was I looking for something?" he asked.

Eidel crossed her arms with a hot expression. That woke him up more than even a blinding-bright sunrise could.

"Oh! Oh, oh. Yes, yes, yes. Yes, I found-I found some things. I did find out something."

"Well?" she asked.

"Uh," Baxter began. He crouched down and shut the book slowly, with hesitation, and let it rest. "Well, I understand the general nature of what happened to your father now," Baxter explained. "I think, perhaps, it was part of a sort of exchange between him and the Shade whom he contracted with to—"

"Contracted?" Eidel repeated. "It's a curse, is it not?"

"It is," Baxter said uncertainly. "But it's not supposed to be. The way it's been handled, yes, it is a curse. But the way it's explained from this account, it's not so much."

"Well, what does he know?" Eidel asked, pointing down to the book. "A man who survived meeting these monsters had to have some way of undoing their spell on his mind or he wouldn't have the mind left to write a book that long, would he?"

"Most of it was written at the time of discovery," Baxter said. She wasn't having his semantic dissension, and he sighed. "It creates a suggestion," Baxter explained, "within the recipient's mind. It implants knowledge and informs the recipient of what that knowledge represents to them along with a reason and intention to follow it. It's not exactly a curse as much as it is…. How can I explain this? It's as though the knowledge gained was always there, and only then is it given purpose."

"Find out," Eidel said, "by tomorrow if it can be lifted and how. That's all I care about. The history and the legacy of this curse and these cursed Shade monsters can be eaten by moths and bookworms and forgotten for good after that."

"Well, I'd like that not to happen," Baxter politely protested.

Derek pulled himself up onto the carriage and saw the end of the exchange, at which point Eidel hopped over the front and assumed her position at the rider's mount.

Baxter sighed and started pushing the book up to a safer position with the feed bags and the bundled-up tarp to keep it from sliding away. Then he sat on it for security.

"We'll be at Galiley today, yeah?" Derek asked.

"Should be," Eidel said. "By morning, at least."

"Then it's off to the Old World," Derek announced, "and follow the map there to the Shades' home." He pointed under Baxter to the book.

Baxter took it upon himself to speak on the book's behalf.

"I think the closest place we could leave from to follow this journey league for league," he explained, "would be Shish."

"Sounds fun!" Derek said.

"If Shish still exists," Baxter said. "The accounts of this book are ancient, mind you. It's written in relatively common words, but—"

"Hee-ohh!" Eidel shouted. She whipped the reins, and the horses both bucked up and stirred into motion. The carriage jerked forward and sent both boys in the back scrambling for balance for a moment. Once the carriage was in full motion down the road, the boys managed to steady themselves.

"Sorry, what were you saying?" Derek asked, shouting over the sound of the clattering wheels and the hoofbeats of the horses.

"We'll just have to see what happens when we get there," Baxter said. "Leaving for the Old World countries isn't exactly easy. Even for a credible Porter."

"Well, we're in luck," Eidel shouted back. "Galiley is bound to be full of credible Porters, so you two rich boys will have no issue clearing out all the paperwork that lets you take part in something as illicit as live-cargo hauling across the Empire's borders."

"I thought you were a Porter," Derek yelled. She didn't answer, letting her own snide remark about their lack of gratuity linger. He turned to Baxter in confusion.

After a moment of considering whether to continue the exchange or simply let it lie in her favor, he relented with a roll of his eyes. "We'll figure it out—if, even on my Master's name, we find someone who can take us in."

"Or at the least," Eidel grumbled to herself, "we can sell off this gaudy, awful cart."

They proceeded through the rest of the wilderness in relative silence. The rattle of the wheels accompanied their travel as they went over the well-worn road, on and off the stone-laid segments, and back into the wilds again. Their travel took them through a long, mostly thin forest just as the night began in earnest. The clouds were few and distant, and the stars were plentiful. The moon wouldn't help them under the shadows of the trees, however. The land was rife for ambush, and their enemies were still in pursuit.

"Hey," Derek called. "So, those Shades…. Did you read any more on how to fight them?"

"The author didn't fight them," Baxter said. "They weren't his enemies, it seems. He was invited to their land and shown the way through the inner markings that they made into his mind."

"So, how'd he survive then?" Derek asked.

"That's a perfectly valid question," Baxter said, "that, hopefully, he was lucid enough to remember and intelligent enough to explain. And perhaps also artful enough at the end of his journey to draw properly."

The carriage continued its rattling roar through the woodlands. The trees caught and dampened the loud, echoing noise of the horses and studded wheels as they made time in a sprint through the winding, turning forest road. It wasn't built for convenience as was the rest of the trade path; it was built for function over the flattest parts of the forest that needed the least work done to make it wide enough to allow for carts and carriages to pass through. The lane was just wide enough for two, but not quite wide enough for their foreign design to fit another past it.

They also rode by lantern light alone. Their most precious resource in defending their wares was light against the shadowy fiends, but it created a stage for other potential hostile elements to find them. A proper Night Porter knew to never take long rides by lantern light. A bandit who heard a horse would be called a fool, but a bandit who spotted a rider carrying a lantern on horseback would be given first cut of the plunder stolen from the rider. Even with the defenses of their cart, their horses were unarmored and vulnerable to attack. Eidel stayed wary of every possible avenue of danger, down to the last shadow her lantern cast against the trees.

The night wore on, long and uneventful. Boredom in the day was meant to be fixed with work or movement, but boredom at night only had one great solution. Baxter was already undertaking it and slept while sitting up in the corner. His dead weight kept the book in place, and the oat bags kept him from sliding around too much.

Derek stayed awake and sat as a vanguard, staring mostly out of the side or front of the carriage. Watching the environment coming in was easier than watching it speed away. When his eyes and stomach failed to match the motions and he grew agitated, he would just stare down at the floor until his upset innards were quelled. On rare occasions, he would turn toward the back and give it a glance as well. Just long enough to see if anything was running behind them or climbing up the back.

And there was. A long, reaching hand gripped hard against the grain of the carriage as its body hung desperately out the back. The silent infiltrator, covered in dark, reached blindly around at the rear for something to grab along the sides. Its long, spindly fingers found one of the ruts in the wagon bed that held the axle of the rear wheel, and it gripped it hard. Derek deftly ignored his nausea and was propelled by adrenaline. He slid back rapidly with his foot up and stomped the hand that grabbed at the siding.

The Shade opened its mouth with a loud, phantasmal gasp. Derek's foot was braced in one place, so he used the other to give a stern kick to its head. It flinched from the impact, but its arm still held on tight to the back and refused to budge. Derek kicked at it again, hitting the top of its head. It ignored the pain and pressed forward, inching itself along as it climbed up the horizontal plane. Derek shook his leg and gave it another kick. Just then, the carriage hit a bump, and both he and the monster were sent off the solid back for an instant. Derek felt himself falling. Things slowed down around him.

He'd been in such a situation before and knew how to react properly. First, he turned and reached for the same place the Shade once held onto, as it had proven to be a proper handhold. He shot his arm out and stiffened it before he bounced back against the surface again. The Shade went tumbling onto the road far back as the carriage sped away. Derek grabbed the side and hit the floor. The bounce combined with the speed of their travel caused him to start falling out of the unguarded back, but his strong grip on the side kept him in. He was hanging on with one arm as his legs dangled out and nearly touched the speeding ground. With a loud groan he pulled himself back up and crawled on his belly the rest of the way to the front of the cart.

"Did you fall out?" Eidel shouted, tilting her head to the side.

"No," Derek answered. "Not quite."

"Stay alert," she said. "There could be anything out here."

"Could be, yeah," he agreed. He was left panting with worry. As the adrenaline wore off, the sickness returned, and he held his head over the side, looking forward, just in case. He kept glancing back for just moments at a time, but no more Shades attacked them. Once they exited the forest, he relaxed his guard a bit. Before them were long, reaching plains and prairies with odd spots of darkness where the clouds smudged over the lights in the sky.

The horses slowed to a trot. Their long run was over, along with the forest behind them, though Derek remained on the defensive. He kept trying to scan the horizon behind them for as long as his stomach would allow him but didn't spot any similar moving shadows coming up from the distance. The horses started lugging the cart up the long, slight grade of a hill. On their way up, another wagon passed by. Four horses pulled it at a gallop down the slope, and it had a fully stocked and covered load of goods in the back. Derek just heard the driver call out to slow his horses as his wheels began digging out dirt just off the road.

"We're almost there," Eidel shouted. "Get yourselves presentable. You'll have to sit up here with me once we get close."

"Why's that?" Derek asked. He noticed Baxter was fully slumped over with his head resting halfway in the partially open bag of feed. He had crumbs and other edible detritus in his hair.

"Human cargo is illegal," Eidel explained, "without the right kind of cart or carrying permits. I'm not even technically a Night Porter. So, they're going to stop us no matter what to ask what kind of a job I'm on. You'll both have to come up and stage yourselves as my bodyguards."

"Well that's a given for me," Derek said, "but Baxy can't even guard his own body, mostly. What's he here for if that lie doesn't pan out?"

"I doubt they'll care enough," Eidel said. "They only talk to Porters, so you two are better off staying quiet. The worst thing they could do is take the cart for inspection. We'd never get it back—not that I care—but they might take the book as well if they think it's a good we aim to sell."

"We can hide it, then," Derek said. He crawled over and slapped Baxter on the shoulder to wake him up, crumb-hair and all. Baxter darted his head around, throwing a light dusting of feed in all directions as he sat up straight and immediately checked under his hips for the book again.

"There it is," Eidel announced. The boys both turned and faced forward on either side of the wagon. From the peak of the hill, they could see the road that sloped down gently across the rest of the journey, past groves and around sharp hills and over a river two times before town. Galiley, the City of Stars, sat over a major river tributary where several minor rivers fed from deep mountain springs, and floodplains joined up to form the Starlook River, which led out to the sea and formed the formal boundary between the High World Empire and the Old World countries.

The city itself was a bastion against the darkness, brightly lit even in the dead of night and visible from miles away. The horses began a gentle trot downward along the remainder of the trade road, where other shimmering lights of night-going travelers came up the way they were going. Baxter kept his hand close over the book to keep it steady and safe. A new city, with new people, and new ways for their enemies to interrupt their important mission was ahead….

<h1 style="text-align:center">15</h1>

The sun was still not close to rising, but the night was officially over. As soon as the carriage drew under the guardian lights of Galiley, up close to its impressive walls, the ancient bastion force against the invading forces of the Old World's wars, the riders all felt much safer. Eidel guided the horses into a smooth entry along the trading line at the west entrance. Derek sat at her left, arms crossed, looking tough, while Baxter had reversed his waist-high cloak to his front and held the book up in his lap to give him the broad, square appearance of a barrel-chested, stronger man.

Two armored guards wielding long spears waited out in front of the main gatehouse. The passage into the city was a full carriage length and more. The walls were thicker than those of most houses, at least in Checcheri. Such was its part in ancient history, a city that had withstood a hundred wars, as eternal as the starlight. The major trade hub ran all sorts of cargo from one place to another. It was on the edge of

Vincia, between two other major city-states on the safest roads available. Every entrance, on ground or over water, had to boast the same protection, which had kept it a stable place for many generations.

"Hold," the guards ordered. One moved in front of Eidel's horses and picked up a handful of hashed feed from a satchel around his waist. The other approached the riders while the horses were distracted with the offered feed. Baxter couldn't help but exchange a look with the approaching guard before forcing his eyes forward again.

"Hello, sir," Eidel greeted. She stuck out her chest a bit so the Porter Guild sigil on it showed more prominently. The guard looked it over and turned his attention to her instead of the square fellow near him.

"Night Porting?" he asked.

"Yes, sir," she answered. "On a return from Checcheri, as it happens."

The guard stepped back and looked over the war wagon. "Odd cart," he remarked.

"It's the cargo," she said. "Partially used, old custom rig from a noble. The top was taken off and transferred onto a newer base for use riding out to the twin burgs of Mikel and Gello."

The guard tapped a stiff, heavily lacquered, and compacted club against the metal wheel studs. "Nobles have such tastes," he muttered. He hooked his boot on the wheel spoke and peeked inside the back. There was nothing left but the tarp and the feed. Not even space for their own traveling provisions. "You came here light."

"It's a nobleman's job," Eidel said. "Not much time to stay idle in the walls."

"All right," the guard sighed. "If you're heading to trade out the cart, you'll need to take it to the Porter's Guild directly. That's along the main street, on the West Bank. Don't take this over the First Bridge. No trade goes on over there."

"Yes, sir," she replied.

"What about the horses?" Derek quietly asked. Eidel shushed him with a curt, aggressive face, then softened her expression immediately when she turned back to the guard.

"Does the Guild require a deposit for stabling?" she asked.

The guard gave her and Derek a stern look. Her forced, winning smile combined with his utterly ambivalent vapidness didn't pique his interest or curiosity. The only real mystery staring him in the face was Baxter, who kept his eyes straight ahead without looking at anyone or anything in particular. The weight of the book on his lap was starting to pain his legs. His feet were jittering nervously.

"What about them?" the guard asked, gesturing at Eidel's companions.

"Guards," she answered quickly.

The gate guard arched an eyebrow at her.

She leaned in and rolled her eyes. "Nobleman's job," she repeated.

He rolled his eyes back and nodded.

"Straight on," he instructed. The other guard gave the horses quick pats on the nose and left their path. Once Eidel got them moving, the horses trotted past the overhanging gateway. The three travelers were inside the city at last, surrounded by burning streetlamps and light posts hanging over dozens of shops that lined the main road. Even further out, the lights persisted deep into the town. Though it was closer to morning than night, the city seemed to have an energy, a quality of sleeplessness that they all seemed to empathize with after their harrowing, night-long travels.

"It's flat, 'innit?" Derek asked, glancing over the city.

"It was built on a river," Eidel explained.

"Originally," Baxter added as he grunted to reposition the book flat against his legs instead of propping it up on its spine, which distributed its massive weight and allowed the blood to rush uninhibited to his feet once more. "Galiley was two cities separated by the river. Both laid claim to it and fought for a while until the Age of Conquest began. Oddly enough, that shift of the global paradigms forced them to ally together, and both sides collaborated on the construction of the First Bridge, which united them, and the River of Stone, which is the wall that protected them."

"Was all that information in there?" Eidel asked, motioning to the square protrusion under his cloak.

"No," Baxter said, "in a different book I read."

"You've read every book there is, haven't you?" Derek asked. He nudged Eidel with his elbow. "He's planning to be the Master Archivist someday, this one. He's probably read more than anyone working at the Merchants' Guilds combined."

"Merchant workers are some of our main clients at the Archive," Baxter mentioned. He looked away, a bit bashful and distant, with a hollow smile on his face. "Being a Master Archivist is about more than just reading books, though…."

Eidel could tell that the distance between his words meant about as much as her own reluctant silence about her father. Derek could tell the same, but he still decided to awkwardly add, "Well, that, and the old one's not gonna, um…be healthy anymore."

"Shh!" Eidel hissed.

Derek ducked his head in apology. They rode the cart up to the entrance of the main Porter's Guild hall, a massive barn of many carts and carriages, some of which were still waiting their turn in a long line of standing horses. Most of these vehicles stood empty, though many within were being stocked up with trade bound for one city or another. Eidel disembarked as did her companions. Baxter lowered himself first and hauled the book up over his shoulder second until Derek rounded the horses and took the book with an affirmative nod.

"I'm going to try and hock this piece of junk fast," Eidel said, slapping the side of the wagon. "You two guard the horses. If someone asks you to move, tell them to jump in the river."

"Is that part of the customs here?" Derek quietly asked Baxter.

"As far as modern customs go," Baxter said, "we should just keep our heads down. We're not exactly tourists or fair-weather travelers. We're on a mission that's a bit more...improper toward the Empire's ideals surrounding trade agreements."

Derek nodded, then squinted. "Oh...illegal," he realized.

Baxter nodded and put his finger to his mouth. Derek caught on and nodded back. "That'll be half our fight already. We can just be glad we don't have to deal with fighting off Shades while we're here."

"Yeah," Derek said. "Unless the ones that almost caught us in the forest followed us here."

A long silence passed between them. During that time, Baxter went through a range of emotion that mostly consisted of different levels of disappointment and confusion. He rubbed his eyes, pinched the bridge of his nose, shook his head, took a deep breath, and then sighed it out. Finally, he turned back to Derek with a single pertinent question. "And?"

"Hmm?" Derek said with a glance. "Oh…and I won."

"Well, good," Baxter sighed. After their silence, Eidel came back with a tall, hunched man. Baxter quickly undid his robe and handed it up to Derek. "Hide the book."

Derek was confused for a moment until Baxter pointed to his eyes. He nodded and bound it up as best he could so no part of it was visible, even in his grasp.

"Let's take a look," the man muttered, eyeing their cart.

Eidel rejoined Derek and Baxter at the side of their carriage and scanned the area they were in quickly. The sky above was still dark but rimmed on all sides with burning lights. The brightness of the city didn't preclude it from having shadowy places, though. As she looked around, something caught her eye, a glimmer of metal somewhere out of the light and public view. Then, as she looked its way, it vanished.

"Baxter," she whispered. He saw her tilt her head slightly behind her and followed her gesture. He hid his own look by crossing his arms and moving his mouth in mock conversation with her.

"What are you doing?" she asked, confused by his puzzling behavior.

"I see it too," he said between silent mouth movements. "Are there usually bandits that bold in this city?"

"Around the Porter Guild maybe," she answered.

"Then who should we tell?" he asked.

Derek bluntly turned fully around and looked down the street. He saw someone shadowy observing them who then vanished behind a wall and into the unlit back alleys of the city. Eidel grabbed at his arm, but Derek didn't budge.

"Did you see him?" Baxter asked, skipping over all admonishment for Derek's lack of stealth, knowing it would do no good. Besides, they had more pressing things to handle at the moment.

"Just a bit," Derek muttered. "But out here, it could be anyone or anything."

"You said the Shades already followed us out to the forest," Baxter reminded him, to Eidel's shock. "Did it look like—?"

"No, no," Derek said. "He didn't have the, uh," he motioned his fingers up over his head to indicate the headpiece mantle the Shade Lord wore. "I think it was just a person, but they were looking at us."

The man came up on them, forcing Eidel to turn around first. "So, this cart," he began, "I don't see no insignias of any noble house or fraternity or other Guild. Not even a Porter's symbol. Can you explain again how you came upon it?"

"Well, sir," Eidel began, complacent and timid as the nature of her job required. Baxter, however, could see the man was a shrewd and prudent sort of broker who wouldn't accept even well-constructed lies. He was a tough and ugly man with a forehead and chin both rounded and bulbous around his face. He had no sympathy in his soul to tug at whatsoever. He reminded Baxter of a nobleman, so used to being in the right that his own errors had to be faulted to someone else. The kind of man who'd make the victim of a scam done on his trade apologize unless they could force it back in the corrupt broker's face.

"It belonged," Baxter explained, "to a group of assassins who snuck into Checcheri from a consortium out of the Old World to attempt to attack the Master Archivist under the cover of night."

The man stared down in anger at Baxter and unfolded his crossed arms in a threatening stance.

Derek stepped forward, one arm occupied with the concealed book, and equalized his threat with nothing more than a look.

"They used, and by that, I mean threatened," Baxter continued, "a local minor Porter house within the city to gain entry under the premise of Old World pottery as crafts trades, which I believe, so long as the wares were found empty and otherwise unladen with contraband contents, are within the trade accords to be processed between the city-states. That fraud had to pass through one checkpoint to come to our city's gates.

"How they managed to slip by an inattentive and mostly vacuous system is well within my understanding, as a civil servant connected to the noble houses who manage the gates. What I want to know, Sir Guildsman, is how such a thing came across that bridge and through this aisle of trade. And how in only the span of a few days you managed to seemingly forget the sight of this unique craft and yet still recall enough to know exactly where to inspect it to find a seal of ownership."

The man realized he was cornered and let out a huff. He couldn't silence Baxter's astute observations of his own neglect, willful or otherwise, without causing a scene with Derek, and he couldn't fashion a retort after having already been proven in the wrong. Even if he had authority and credibility in the city to back him up, the threat of noble interference made him hesitate.

"So, you'll have me buy this back," the Guildsman slowly reasoned out, "and corroborate with your use of illegal wares?"

"No," Baxter corrected. "You're going to buy our silence." That infuriated him. "As an apprentice of the Master Archivist, I am quite an avid reader, enough to also be a very skilled Scribe. I don't even need a copyhouse to help me. From now until morning, if I write uninterrupted, I can wallpaper all of this street with a detailed admission of these events and your participation in them. We are merely victims of this crime. We merely used the contraband to escape the very deviants who used it to cross illegally and commit illicit deeds. You, sir, willingly passed them through."

"You lying, talking, reading…." The man seemed to exhaust his supply of abject put-downs after that and relented in a huff. "Fie on you, then." He reached around his back to a satchel purse and pulled out a fistful of uncounted coins. He tossed them at Baxter and let them bounce off his chest as a final act of spite. "Then, I'll pay you for the firewood." He glanced at their cart bitterly. "Thank you and goodbye!" He stomped away and left Baxter and Eidel to tend to the coins on the ground. They waited until he was clearly out of sight before they both bent down and scraped them up into their hands.

"Does this look like it was worth it?" Baxter asked.

"Worth what?" Eidel asked, angrily. "My pride?"

"I'm sorry," Baxter replied as snippy as he could be. "I just didn't think your plan to convince him to buy an unmarked, foreign war wagon with nice words was going to work. I should have had more confidence in you. Shame on me!"

"He's watching us again," Derek said. Baxter and Eidel stopped bickering and locked eyes. "He's not hiding, either."

Baxter looked back and saw the man, all covered in shadows, standing in the street. While they all stood and crouched, a cart pulled out from the barn and made its way down the road the man stood on. When it passed by, he disappeared once more into the darkness like a shadow chased away by the light….

16

The back streets and alleyways of West Galiley were home to a network of criminals; the corruption ran so deep it spanned the whole city. Otherwise innocent bystanders, people who milled their days away in the constant struggle of working-class drudgery, took to the dark walks of the late night and early morning as a means to quell their wanting hearts. Ordinary citizens and passing merchants were tempted by the lawless side of the city, but never got lost in it. They just dipped their feet in the dark waters and convinced themselves it was a fling or a fancy. And there were those who made a profit from their indiscretions.

In the dark halls made up of the backs and sides of buildings, some of which opened out to no street but instead functioned as hiding places for such dark deeds and their doers to assemble, the traders of the night made their routes, selling goods and services no Porter would carry and no Merchant would handle.

Some carried nothing more than the blade they owned.

One man stalked his way through the alleys under the dark cover of a hood and cloak with something shining in his hand. Others ignored and avoided him. He had his business, and no one had business that stopped him. He maneuvered to stay parallel with the road, which connected to the main one, which in turn led to the First Bridge and dipped back to the surface road, and he peeked down that way. He saw nothing he was looking for; so, he turned around, seeing only carts moving out before the first light came. Whatever he was looking for had evaded him, at least for now.

He was about to turn away from the street when he spotted one of his marks hoisting a package under his arm. It was the smallest one, relatively. Not the thick, muscular brute or the waifish but sturdy-looking girl. The thin one who talked enough to get himself out of trouble. The smart one, obviously. The man in shadows stayed hidden as the boy approached on a power walk down the street. He kept something tucked close to his side under his arm: a bundle of robes in a nearly square shape.

The man in the shadows kept to the alleys and followed the thin one's path to the next side street over. The one he followed looked lost and confused, wandering aimlessly down a road that had no end or purpose for his venture, one that split toward the riverbank road of commerce and trade on one side, and on the other, down along the wall side where the worst crimes occurred under the blind spot of the rampart watch. He was an easy pick for sure. The boy stood out in the open and looked around, separated from his friends.

The man started to make his move. The shining metal in his hand retreated slowly into his cloak. He kept his head low so even the streetlights had a difficult time reaching his face. While the boy's back was turned, he approached, one hand reaching toward his shoulder to grip him and turn him around.

The shadow-coated man was felled by a stiff strike to the back of the head. Derek had managed to get behind him and bring the broad side of the *Daemondimonium* down on top of his hooded head while Baxter served as a tantalizing distraction. The man crumpled to the ground and dropped his tool, pawing at his head desperately. Seeming to realize he was not in lethal danger, the cloaked man quickly scrambled up to his feet. In the meantime, Baxter tossed his cloak over and Derek covered the book up again.

"You should watch yourself," Baxter said sarcastically. "I heard there's crime in these parts."

The man stumbled to a stop, under the light and fully exposed, looking every inch the proverbial stalker. He had an inherently untrustworthy face: round and boyish but marred by scars and age. His hair was thin all over and bunched up on top of his head in a frontward, wispy spike. He was missing a few teeth in his crooked, pleading smile, and his eyes shimmered deep blue.

"Wh-wha-what's the trouble here?" he asked in a lilting voice as if he'd just stumbled onto them that instant. "Do we gots some kind of-of problem out here? Are you…are you both lost or something?"

Baxter reached down and retrieved the man's item. It was a round-tipped, broad, and edgeless thing, like a very long and narrow metal mirror or some kind of comically large, glossy file. "Were you planning to…spread butter all over me with this?"

"That's a quick mason spreader," Derek said. He glanced at it again as Baxter displayed it with a turn of his wrist. "A fancy one."

"No, no, naw, naw, naw," the man protested. He reached forward with a grasping hand and approached, but Derek held him back by simply raising the covered book up as if to strike him once more. "C'mon, mates. You're getting this all wrong!"

"We did get one thing wrong," Baxter agreed, "in that this isn't a knife or sword. But you were stalking me and took an opportunity when my back was turned to approach me unseen and unheard."

"But what you didn't expect," Derek proudly added, "was for us to be hiding nearby and…. Oh, wait, where's Eidel?"

"Eidel, come out!" Baxter shouted. She emerged from a nearby alleyway holding a riding crop in one hand, which she tapped against the other.

"Right, right," the man began. "Of course, you're confused. I'm sorry for the belligerence in my actions, but I assure you, as sure as my beamer is polished, that my intentions were in no way matching my obvious descript nature."

Eidel moved toward the others and inspected the metal object. She looked at him suspiciously. "Are you supposed to be a civil worker?"

"This is a civil worker's tool?" Baxter asked.

"That it is," the man said. "And I'd like to do you the kindness of showing its usage to you, if you wouldn't mind?"

Baxter looked at Eidel, who hesitantly nodded. He handed it over, and the man held it up over his head. He managed to catch the light of a nearby lamp and reflected it up to a slightly concave point at the tip of the mirrored edge to shine a beam of light upon a nearby building.

"Less fuel than a lantern," he said, "and many times brighter. Now, sirs and madam, allow me the honor. I am Goffee, a hired guide by the Galiley guardsmen to show those passing through or wandering their way around town to their destinations 'ere or across the Starlook River."

"A guide?" Baxter scoffed. "What guide stalks a group of three from the shadows and approaches one from behind like you did?"

"Well, one well-versed with these streets," Goffee retorted. "It's part of the customs 'round here. One caught thieving by another with intent to thieve won't press onto a man already marked. Especially at night, in these dead hours before the sunrise, one must adapt to the dark and not expose oneself until it's safe enough."

"So, it's safer to fake a robbery," Baxter complained, "than to just wave me down to offer your service?"

"'Round here, yes, sir," Goffee plainly answered. Baxter turned to Eidel again, but she could only shrug.

"That sounds right," Derek said. They both turned to him for further explanation. "It's like what we did in the union. We hung around a place needing work and pretended to be on break so no one else would come to start fixing it without us getting paid. They thought someone was already working there and moved along."

"That sounds less dishonest than thieving," Baxter said.

"Rest assured, sirs and madam," Goffee said, "I am no thief. Else I'd carry an honest blade, and you may check my person if you would like to find one, but I've none to find."

"That's all right," Baxter said. "So, then, is it pure philanthropy that gives you a cause, or will you extract payment in some way once your tour is done?"

"No, sir, no," Goffee politely protested. "I respect your frankness, though, so I will inform you, yes, my services are paid ones, but you aren't the ones who pay it. I'm employed by an under-net of secret handshakes among the Merchant Guilds in the city to keep travelers safe from the unchecked crime that stalks the streets in earnest."

"Why can't the guards do this?" Eidel asked. "Why you? Why this way?"

"The guards," Goffee began a bit darkly, "are as to Galiley as the nobles are to other city-states. They hold authority upon the rampart watch where they can look down over all without repercussion. None may enter or leave without their hands being wet with the waters of their trade, you see. The Porters and Traders all give unfair shares to the guards lest they be removed by force from their rented homes."

Eidel looked to Baxter for approval. Baxter thought back along to what he learned about Galiley's history, but none of it was modern. Passing letters and noble decrees between cities weren't managed by the Archive. "I say," Baxter began, "we at least address him honestly and see what he has to offer us in the way of a tour."

"There's only one thing," Eidel quietly complained, "that we're after, and no tour guide will show it to us."

"Then how…?" Baxter whispered back.

"Leave that to me," she said. "I can speak with other Porters about—"

"Alone?" Baxter interrupted. "Are you sure?"

"I didn't ask you for help," she whispered harshly. "You step on my toes too much and unbalance me. I don't need that to do my own business."

"Have you ever spoken with someone connected to human cargo before?" he shot back. She didn't answer, and he half-opened his mouth to make an additional quip but relented. Their conversation ended before they had stopped talking, so Baxter turned back to the waiting Goffee instead. "We've traveled all night," Baxter declared, "and could use a rest through the morning. We aim to move through night travel and need to find and speak with professional Porters before their contracts all get filled."

"Then you've come at a good time," Goffee announced, "and on a good day and to a good place. This is the link of chains between the two living worlds. The High World values the foreign market trade and the ease of access to the Starlook River's port to the northbound current, while the Old World enjoys similar benefits from further south and upriver to connect with the Vincian states."

"That just so happens to concern us," Baxter said. "We're looking for someone to take us to the Old World as soon as possible."

"That's possible," Goffee agreed. "It is possible to arrive anywhere if one starts in the city of Galiley. Come. Follow. Let me instruct you. You shall want no more for history or lawful knowledge of this place once the sun has risen over the eastern rampart of the River of Stone. Please follow me if you will. I shall conclude our tour, as a gratuity, at an inn with vacancies for your weary, hard-traveled bodies."

Goffee stood and waited for them all to agree. Baxter seemed tentative on following through but moved forward nonetheless. Derek joined him without question. If any problems arose, Derek seemed sure that he'd know how to solve them, or at least sufficiently quell them. Eidel had no other option and followed after them but kept her distance in the group, never standing closer to Goffee than

Derek did for protection. Out of all the muggers and thieves and potential real criminals in the streets, Goffee seemed the most duplicitous and untrustworthy.

Despite their awful first impression, Goffee stuck to his word as a tour guide. He led them through the western half, even through the dark alleys, without worry. For those places, he shined a bright beam down the path he chose to take, and any nasty elements lying in wait would casually flee the scene. If he wanted, he explained he could aim the light straight up or toward the ramparts. Just one flash would be enough to bring the guards swarming into the area within minutes. That was the system in which he worked. He was connected to the guards, and by their authority, he was given free rein to keep travelers safe just by being near them.

He guided them down the main street they had ridden in on and highlighted all the best places for their various needs, including traveling provisions and horse equipment. They avoided the gatehouse and instead traveled into a residential market section with shops just beginning to open and start up their street-side vendor stations. Fresh-cooked food and freshly imported food from Old World traders were on offer at every stop, all temptations to loosen their combined purse strings.

Once the westside had been adequately toured, they crossed the First Bridge together. It was as wide and impressive as the main street itself, arching up on a sloping grade but still tall enough that the first morning longboats came in from upriver with their companies rowing to the beat of tired boating songs. The ports of trade were all along the riverfront and occupied most of the constructed riverbanks.

On the eastside, historically part of the Old World, everything was different. The more modern architecture they were used to was behind them. What remained were the humble, wide-spread abodes made of stone and rock and dried plaster sealant extending in every direction and even layered on top of each other. The Old World builders cared not for decadence, only for efficiency of space.

Each block was like a castle of homes connected to other homes. Row houses that rose three or four stories high were the norm. The continuation of the main street featured mostly houses, and all the trading posts and ports were closer to the other ancient, massive gatehouse that faced the open scrublands in the distance. Behind them was greenery and an abundance of forest lands, but ahead were simpler lands. Forests were rare and thin, but pastures and farms were far larger and well-populated with livestock. Their two worlds met over the banks of the Starlook River and shook hands in trade and peaceful unity.

"It seems so easy," Baxter said. "Like we could just…walk right out of the gate from here."

"So, why don't we?" Derek asked.

"No sane person would enter trade," Eidel said, "on foot into the badlands. Even on horseback. We either need a cart and trade of our own or to be taken as the cargo of someone else."

"Pardon," Goffee said, standing silently behind them until he spoke, becoming part of their hidden and questionably legal conversation. "If the sirs and madam are looking for a way to enter the Old World trade routes…this is something I can also guide you toward."

"Even against the better judgment of your job?" Eidel asked. Goffee smiled, and it sickened her.

"What's a dishonest day of work," Goffee asked, "for a thief, anyway?" All three felt a shiver of regret in trusting him, but they were too far immersed in their plan to turn away even a nefarious hand for help. He was not a Shade and knew what they couldn't ask a typical law-abiding person. That was reason enough for them to follow him into an alley and enter the underworld just as the sun rose and the day truly began.

All the night shadows over the Starlook River were now gone. What remained were the equally dark and dismal shadows of the day….

17

Goffee led the group into a bar, one unlike any of the other readily available drinking establishments in the area. It was off the main road, off the trade routes, and on the side of the city where bars were infrequent. It was an under-the-table establishment in every way, not set up to host customers but rather hide them. Every booth and table seemed to be miserably cramped, so much so that nothing more than a single mug could fit on either side. A place where one-on-one trade and gifts and favors were exchanged and the drinks were simply an afterthought.

It was the perfect place to find someone to trade with in an illicit business, and unfortunately, that was just the place they all wanted to be at the moment. "Sirs and madam," Goffee began, keeping his tone very low and polite, "if you'd like, I can inquire for you, as a patron and member of this establishment, as to what prices are yet open for the journey you are about to undertake."

"We'd appreciate it," Baxter said.

Goffee nodded and bowed, then approached the barkeep, who stood watch over the floor like a sentry with mugs instead of swords and shields. While they had a hidden conversation, half of which was done with fast movements of their hands and fingers moving together to form symbolic gestures, the three leaned up against a far wall and watched.

"This is a far cry from the Porter's Guild," Baxter whispered.

"The Porter's Guild would run us out of the city," Eidel said, "if they knew how we came here or why we have to go as we do."

"At least it'd be fair," Baxter said. "Anyone up to transport us across the way will take us for criminals without a second thought and thieve us with the price."

"I have a thought," Derek offered. They both turned to him in their own unique, judging way, and he sank back against the wall, clamping his mouth shut.

"I think our better bet right now," Baxter decided, "would be to buy our way into work on a caravan."

"How is that better?" Eidel asked.

"They could shelter us and feed us in exchange for our work," Baxter said.

Derek nodded and pointed to him.

"And they'd move in the day," she said, "and stop at night—the exact opposite of the travel we have to make."

"Oh," Baxter realized.

"Night Porters don't make these long trips," Eidel explained, "without extreme compensation for the danger. Selling Derek's muscle as a guard won't be quite enough to make them sprint for the whole four-day journey to the nearest trading town in the Old World."

"Which should be Braat," Baxter said. "Or…or not."

"I thought it was Shish," Derek said. A few people noticed him speaking up, either because of the sharp S sounds he made in the relatively silent bar or because of the word he uttered. They all noticed that many eyes were glaring their way, seeing them fairly as the strangers they were. Not just strange but out of place. They did not belong in this dark, immoral place.

Goffee returned at last and without a word ushered the three out the door and back into the street, leaving just a short peak of light from the curtain over the doorway as they exited. "I guess we're not on their shortlist for travel, then?" Baxter asked.

"Yes," Goffee said. "That is to say, uh, no. It seems no one is making runs from this, uh, hall at the moment to the Old World due to news of traveling brigands and raiders that are sweeping the entirety of the Old World countries and plunging them into a sudden upswing of war." He shrugged, as though that was simply the nature of business.

Eidel turned to Baxter with a worried look. She'd never even heard of wars or brigands with bands large enough to destabilize countries, and if anyone could assuage her doubts over their quest, she wanted it to be him. Baxter, however, looked similarly displeased with the news and gazed up at Derek instead.

"Well," Derek said, "onto the next, then?" He looked down and calmed both of his friends immediately.

"Goffee," Baxter began, "what precisely went on with your negotiations? Was it a judge-by-appearance sort of deal?"

"Travel's just stricter now," Goffee answered with a shrug. "Might stay that way for a while."

"I mean, how did you introduce us?" Baxter asked more clearly. "As what, travelers? Merchants? Runaways? What was your angle to open this dark, unseen door for us?"

"Oh, right," Goffee said. "They never asked. Just said you were people trying to cross to the Old World, no cargo, money uncertain."

"We should probably count our coins before we keep going," Baxter decided, "lest we get saddled with a riding debt and have to pull whatever cart does accept us."

They gathered everything up and gave it to Eidel to keep on the inside pocket of her Porter's Guild apron. In all, they had three silver ducats and twenty-eight bronze, and not one ounce of gold between them. Such a price was agreeable to Derek but pitiful to Eidel. With that as their basis, they tried to find someone willing to accept passengers at one silver per head while reserving the rest for extra negotiation fees or contractual arrangements to make the trip less terrible.

Goffee obliged them to tour the town until their feet started to drag and their exhaustion wore on them like a heavy, wet blanket over their backs. Baxter was the first to waver, then Eidel, and even Derek grew short-tempered by the total lack of rest, given that he had been the most active during their harrowing escape the prior night. The book began to feel heavy in his arms at last.

"Say, Goffee," Derek began, "you know, I was just thinking, we're putting an awful lot of trust in you out of your own obligation, yeah?"

"Yes, yes," Goffee said. "I am at your service."

"I wouldn't do this much work on the side for someone, even if I was already being paid to help them once," he said. "If you've got the choice, you ought to find someone that'll pay you better for your work."

"Oh, pay is not an issue," Goffee replied. "Pay is guaranteed more often than not in this town. So many traders come through. Even with the Old World route currently closed off, it is an efficient in-between for the cities that border the Empire's lands and make use of the river where things are sent covertly away. If only you were traveling further north, you'd only need a raft and but a moment of clouds to pass under the moonlight on the current."

"Travel has to be by moon," Derek said. "We can only rest in the day, even after we leave."

"That may only delay negotiations further," Goffee told him. He muttered something to himself and waved his wrists around. Derek saw him hiding something, and he reached to grab him by the shoulder. Derek's patience was running out, but not for his friends. "S-sir?" Goffee stuttered.

"Derek, stop," Eidel said. She tapped on his wrist to get him to release their weary guide. "We're all too tired for this."

"Well, if we sleep the night here," Baxter said, "at four bronze a head for beds without sheets and no food, we'll have worse problems than just leaving town by nightfall."

"Hmmm," Derek groaned. His patience was still on the edge of depletion. All he could think about was sleep—and the easiest means of forcing his way forward and out of the east gates to the road ahead.

"Perhaps," Eidel suggested, "we should speak with the Porter's Guild again?"

"I doubt the doorman will be happy to see us back," Baxter muttered.

"You know what I forgot about?" Derek said as his stomach joined the conversation. "We haven't eaten anything real yet, have we?"

"Goffee," Baxter said, "is there no between-house for travelers in Galiley? Someplace with charity, or possibly a church with connections to Checcheri? Our goal through the city happens to be one passed down from a certain person of high-standing in our home city."

"Well," Goffee said, "if nobility is on the line or is of issue of some importance, there may be a place that can service you. But-but they'd need some proof. Some reliable symbol of your heritage there, or at least, of your employ."

Baxter turned to Derek and then to the book he still carried swaddled in his robe. There were no robes like it in design or color or even the length to the mid-back. It was the certifiable, approved dressing of the scholars and Scribes of the Archive of Checcheri, a place recognizable by any traveler within the Vincian Empire.

"We may have something," he said. "But tell us first, what is this place you plan to show us next?"

"Our time is of the essence," Eidel added. "And the reason for our hostilities earlier is that we are being pursued."

Goffee suddenly became less open and less hospitable. He regarded the group again with a more worried expression, his eyes lingering the longest on Derek. "Why?" Goffee asked. "If-if it is not offensive to know, that is."

"An attempt was made on the Master Archivist's life," Baxter admitted, "and I am his sole apprentice. He instructed me to leave the Empire entirely and seek shelter in the Old World until times were safer." That much, at least, was true. He didn't have to say the entire reason why they were traveling. It was too fantastical for a peasant man such as Goffee to believe outright.

"Oh, well," Goffee began, "even with the war going on?"

"I believe it is in our best interest to flee," Baxter said. "Those pursuing us, our enemies…they only move at night and are ruthlessly tenacious."

"They'll even hop up," Derek explained, "on the back of a moving cart to drag you off in the night."

Goffee seemed skeptical but trustworthy, in his way. He was straining to believe their words outright, it seemed. "Hmm. Well, yes, then the Thieves Guild hall may have someone to assist you."

"Even thieves have Guilds," Derek informed Baxter with a dismissive tone.

"I ask you not to look down on them for the name alone," Goffee said. "It is an open secret of Galiley. They are remnants of an order from the Old World that forced wealth from the pockets and hands of the royal houses that hoarded it for themselves out of corrupt greed so the peasantry would not starve or suffer in the underlooked squalors of the lesser cities. To do so made them thieves, but they are gentle folk of high repute who denounce common thugs and protect those unable to protect themselves."

"Now that, I don't believe," Derek said. "Of all the things we've seen and learned, that's the hardest kind of lie to pass by me yet."

"It's not impossible," Baxter protested.

"If thieves had honor, they'd have jobs," Derek disputed adamantly. Baxter and Eidel didn't have the same scruples. Their silent argument stemmed more from their tired minds and desperation. They were at their collective wits' end, with barely anything to show for what they'd gone through in their travels so far, and a single itching worry persisted in Baxter's mind about the true value and worth of their expedition.

"Let's try," Baxter said. Derek glanced down at him. "Just to try, to see. At the worst, we may just have to look for something else at night and defend ourselves as best we can."

"Alright," Derek agreed. "That plan I like better. But sure, let's see if this works out first."

"Excellent," Goffee said. "Don't you worry, either. The Thieves Guild takes passengers across the border frequently. They have a long-standing heritage with similar Guilds abroad in the Old World, the orders and leagues of the undercities. They will see to you fairly and, again, not to judge against the name, they value money enough not to covet it."

"Please take us there," Eidel said. "I feel we're skirting dangerous territory discussing this out in public."

"Follow close," Goffee urged. "There are *Thieves*, and there are thieves in Galiley. I will take you to those who mean you well, but I cannot guarantee that we will avoid those who would mean ill."

"That's their mistake," Derek said. He was out of trust and knew they were out of options. He followed along in the rear, tacitly entrusting Goffee to defend his friends from the front of their procession as they entered the centermost district of buildings in the wide expanse of the Old World side city. It was afternoon. The sun was still high enough to cast light between the buildings, but the underworld alleys were so tight and the buildings so high it made that light dim.

They were in the thick of it, it seemed, with no way out but forward. Goffee led them, finally, to a narrow door, somehow even narrower than all the rest, which opened into a room of total darkness. Once inside, Baxter looked around and discerned the nature of the place: a small, walk-through lobby of sorts, much like the entryway of the Archive but the size of a closet.

The darkness was immediately disconcerting. It was a deliberate dark, shadows acting as walls in open spaces with minimal lighting. A place for those unaccustomed to the sun who chose to hide themselves during all hours until there was no one around to see them leaving. Just entering in the day felt taboo, like walking into the Archive at night.

There were times to come and go, and a certain presence of a place made those times apparent by a feeling deep within. The feeling of the place, the aura, felt all wrong. It was so dead silent it felt wrong to breathe too loudly.

The only one who pushed on unoffended was Derek, whose agitation and self-defense prompted his instincts to overcome any general myopic distortions. If there was space, he moved. If he bumped into something, it would be hurt more than him. Eidel moved with similar confidence but stayed closer to Baxter. If anyone could talk their way out, it would be him, and if he failed, she planned to pull him back with full force and entrust the remainder to Derek.

Goffee finally led them to a room. All they could see of the inside were painted doors standing out against charcoal-blackened walls, darker than shadow itself.

"I'll tell you this," Derek muttered, "you don't dress the place well."

"It's for secrecy," Goffee whispered. "These deals, and what they entail, ordinarily…."

"I understand," Baxter said, "but I'm afraid, in our state, if it's this dark, we might sleep before anyone comes to see us."

"A light would be nice," Eidel agreed.

Goffee rubbed his hands together and nodded as they entered the room. "Of course," he said. "Can't read without light, hmm?" He let the door shut quietly while Baxter stood, wide-awake and terrified.

18

The waiting room was cramped and plush with pelt coverings across deep reclining chairs and benches. It was about as big as Baxter's room from his bed to his desk but was so packed in with things to sit on that it felt like there was no space at all. Just benches and a table and the low, low light of a single hanging candle without a cover dripping its wax off the wick into a silvery platter underneath it. It left an acrid smell of burning wax in the air that wafted throughout the room.

"Eidel," Baxter said, "I need to wear my cloak. Can you hide the book with your apron?"

"We already didn't get away," she reminded him, "with you looking burly wearing it under your clothes. You think these people are so backward in their darkened places they'd see a woman with a square belly and let it slide as normal?"

"To wrap the book in, you mean?" Derek asked Baxter. Eidel was less offended by that but remained obstinate.

"We can't risk showing it to them," Baxter said. "But that cloak is one of a kind. Only we at the Archive have them. If they see me wearing it, they will have to believe I am of legitimate employ there."

"Oh, fine," she grumbled. She tried to stand up and had to lean one knee on the seat while she unfastened the back of her apron over her neck. "Excuse me, boys—a lady is changing. Are you going to just stare at her?"

"Should we sing a song?" Baxter asked. Her glare finally persuaded him to turn away. Derek, ornery as he was, still obeyed, holding the covered book up to his face and looking away toward the door. His ire was thoroughly redirected toward the green hue of the cover. On the other side could be any potential brigand or thief of ill repute they would be forced to entrust their great journey with. He didn't like it and made his protest known to all present.

"I know," Baxter said soothingly to Derek, seeing him tensing up. "But it's this or nothing."

"It's this or my plan," Derek reminded him, "which is to break every Shade skull that we come across and wait until morning again."

"I've got my doubts that'll work," Baxter said. The story of Plattius and his journey with the Shade-man was stuck in his mind, still unread and the knowledge incomplete, along with so many of the strange creatures and rites he'd already undergone in his exploration of their destination, left unchanged since those ancient times.

"All right, here," Eidel said. She held out her apron, one layer removed from her outfit, and stood seemingly ashamed in just her plain, straight dress. Baxter noticed how it changed her form, not having the waist-high ties around her to cinch her clothing closer to her back and belly, but he did not speak. And when he thought it, he looked away, just in case she noticed his expression.

"Right," Derek said. He unwrapped the book and put it on the table for a moment. Baxter took up his cloak again. It was wrinkled in some wrong places and didn't quite hold its regular form, but it was good enough. The apron wrapped around the book and covered every part of it. Derek even made the Porter's Guild symbol present itself on the front end of the book, making it appear like a carefully wrapped official present.

"I'm going to rest my eyes," Eidel said with a powerful yawn. She turned away from the candlelight and seemingly drifted straight to sleep against the corner of two benches meeting along the corners of the wall. Baxter hid his yawn in his hand and leaned back, straining to keep his eyes open.

"You don't think this is just a trap, right?" Derek asked. "Because, if there's any place we can't see, they could just shove some fire in and burn us to death, or something, couldn't they?"

"That's a heinous thought to consider," Baxter said.

"They're thieves, though," Derek reminded him as if that were the perfect defense against any argument Baxter could muster.

"Thief is just a mistranslation," Baxter said. Derek waved his hand around in agitation. "It's more like…reverse taxpayers. They took from the rich and gave the money back to the poor, so they weren't dying under the oppression of tyrants."

"Oh," Derek said.

"Although, actually," Baxter added, "I did read the journal of one such royal financier of a sultan's palace from the Old World. Because they went through so many thefts and lost so much money, they just ended up increasing taxes in different ways, with food or mandatory military service to recruit more militiamen who in turn were paid to hunt and stop the thieves outright. They always found ways to maintain their power, even when money wasn't the primary resource to use."

"Hmm," Derek hummed.

"Shut up," Eidel groaned out the curt and direct command. The boys decided somberly to follow her advice and rested on the table. Derek leaned back with his arms crossed, and Baxter laid his head down on the book. As he did, he was forcibly subjected to smelling the floral scents that came off Eidel's apron. Even on their terrifying journey, somehow, a pleasant scent lingered around her belongings.

After a few precious moments of rest and respite, the door received a knock, and the party took on a visitor. It was Goffee once more. He left the door open for someone to walk through. It was an old man with dark, olive skin and a deep black beard that hung down straight and short off his chin and in a shadow-like cover over his jaw and cheeks. He wore loose garb from the lands to the south, where the desert met the forests and where the sun was far hotter for far longer in the year than the Vincian people experienced.

Baxter stood up first and looked the man over. He had eyes that offered no patience for him or his friends. Baxter could tell they immediately faced an uphill battle of sorts just to negotiate their purpose, let alone their price. He recalled reading about the customs of the Old World and gave a short, polite bow to the man, who responded with a knowing nod.

"This gentleman," Goffee said, "is already prepared to make a run through the long stretch to the town of Braat far into the federated nation. He said he could take you as far as there and no farther for one silver piece each, and he intends to travel through night and day."

"We'll pay you now," Baxter said excitedly. "We have extra money left over. If that could be used for provisions on board to keep your vessel moving, we would gladly give that up as well."

The man scanned the room to look them over. One thing caught his eye—the four-cornered thing in Derek's arms. When Derek saw the man looking, he held it tighter and stared him down.

"You are bringing that?" he asked, his accent stiff but not unpleasant as he pointed to the book.

"We are, yes," Baxter replied. He tugged on his cloak from both sides of the inner hem and looked up with confidence. "This matter we are on concerns the Great Archive at Checcheri regarding the return of an ancient artifact to its homeland deep in the Old World territories as a matter of personal pride and a passing request of the Master Archivist, Lothan."

The mention of the name made the man lift an eyebrow curiously. He observed Baxter's short robe and narrowed his eyes in satisfaction. "I am Yahid," he announced. "Give me your names, please."

They did so, in their own order of most awake to least.

"I am Baxter."

"I'm Derek."

"My name is Eidel."

"Come, travelers," Yahid said. "I shall receive you immediately. We need waste no time." Baxter turned to his friends with a grin as the man left the room ahead of them. They were back out in the blinding dark following after Yahid's white-ish robes immediately and followed Goffee's lead to a hidden chamber that led downward.

"Hold on, now," Derek said. "How're we getting out like this?"

"The caverns," Goffee explained, "helped to entrench the old survivors of the River War, which formed the town of Galiley long ago. Before the fortifications were built and the city was made on the east half of the river, the people who settled here relied on the caves of the dried-out underwater river to make their travels. It leads out of the city, unseen by the River of Stone, with stations only for those committed and known to both the Order and the Guild."

"Only the most trusted thieves," Derek said.

"Or," Baxter corrected, "the most honorable."

Derek scoffed at the remark and followed down after them both. He turned back as he descended slowly to the dark of the room behind him with a bad feeling readable on his dour expression.

"The sun will set soon," Yahid said. "Under the veil of night, we shall be going."

"How long were we asleep?" Baxter wondered quietly.

"Couldn't have been too long," Eidel said. "This crick in my neck is telling me at least two hours."

"Three and a half," Derek said. He turned forward to their curious faces. "When I can't sleep, I pass time in my head by reliving boring jobs. One of them lasts almost exactly ten minutes, and I counted it six, twelve, eighteen, nineteen, twenty…." Derek leaned against the cavern wall and scraped his bare shoulder against the dry rocks for a moment.

"That's extremely impressive," Baxter said. "But you didn't sleep at all?"

"Hehehe," Derek chuckled dryly. He was stumbling like he was drunk, a sight Baxter was used to seeing many times over from his own dysfunctional family. The sight gave him a brief tinge of melancholy.

They finally arrived at a fairly well-lit area, deep enough in the earth to be warm despite the lack of light or sizeable fires. Every candle spread its light out far through thick glass lanterns. People were working, their faces covered by dark sashes and their hands wrung hard with the effort of long periods of stress without rest. Cracked fingernails were signs of hard but unchecked work. They made Baxter flinch as they passed by, undeterred in their march through the carved-out cavern walls.

Finally, they came to the dock of carriages. Some were being unloaded of sensitive objects, jars and satchels full of things that were better left out of either land. Forbidden spices and barred trade goods that were too unlawful to even fine for possession, and many of the carts carrying them were constructed in ways to hide them in compartments within the frame. Eidel recognized some of the makes, with sloping sidewalls in the rear that led up to fancy riding seats in the front made for two horses comfortably and four in desperation. Carrying carts, not for drugs but for people—usually nobles going across the roads to other towns.

Their cart was much simpler. It was half-loaded with barrels and kegs of things. Baxter saw a load of stripped, cured animal legs being lowered into one barrel and whole fish being dunked into the waters of another where they quickly seemed to revive from the moisture and swim in the tight space. A Food Porter between towns seemed innocent enough. Why his business brought him into the Underdark of misery and corruption was unforeseen and unknown.

"The payment," Yahid said, "shall be delivered outside of town."

"Very well," Baxter said. He turned to Eidel and nodded, but she didn't do anything. He looked down at her and realized, again, she wasn't wearing her apron. Then he turned to Derek.

"Oh, right," he said. "I was wondering when I wrapped this why it felt lumpy." They all forgot that she kept their scant resources on the inside pockets of her apron. Derek carefully tried to reach into it but ended up unfurling part of the cover in the process. Yahid watched them intently as they fumbled around. Baxter joined the effort and held the book up while Derek rifled through the many folds of the apron, and Eidel quickly came over to do the most logical thing by removing it outright.

"Here," she said. She hadn't forgotten why they wrapped it up. Derek and Baxter didn't even react at first. Their brief break from danger had made them less careful than before. They exposed the book as they had once desperately tried not to, only to regret it immediately when the first flame in the cavern turned blue. Then another and another, until the only light shining nearby came from the light of Goffee's eyes.

"Ha!" the thief-guide shouted.

Yahid looked on with fret as every thief in the cave, one by one, turned into hissing, blue-eyed creatures with no more sense than reason for violence. Baxter immediately tossed off his cloak and covered up the book from above while it was in Derek's hands. The blue fire was subdued, but not diminished. The lights dimmed from the many thieves' eyes, but their intent remained.

"There it is!" Goffee exclaimed. "I knew I saw it! I knew, so I followed you. I knew, so I tried to ensnare you! I knew, and so, I shall be rewarded for it."

"To hell with the whole lot of you!" Derek shouted. His strong voice echoed through the cavern and filled every tunnel and drive in and out of sight. "You come close, and I'll sink this book fifty pages deep into your skulls!"

"Get on the cart, sir!" Baxter shouted to Yahid. "We're under attack!"

Dozens of blades were drawn, creating a symphonic harmony of metal against sheathes. Yahid ran right to his cart, past some of the criminals that began forming a wall to block the party off. Goffee stepped out in front and tried to smooth back his wispy hair across his head. His eyes were still glowing, not as brightly but still with a sickeningly deep shade of blue.

"It's very fortunate," Goffee said, "that we were able to meet this way. Time after time, I tried to force you away from the light so I could use my power to see through you in the dark. It was pitiful, leading you, lost like lambs, to the back of the barn for the slaughter to commence."

"Looks like I was right," Derek said confidently. "No honor among thieves."

"They're not just thieves anymore," Baxter said. "You…. Did you make contact with a Shade? Did you receive the Gift?"

"Ah," Goffee said, "you know? And yet, you are not imbued. You know not the importance of that tome."

"I know who did this to you," Baxter said. "The fiend, the Shade Lord. What was his name?" He turned to Eidel, whose anger was rapidly mounting.

She threw her apron down, money and all, and reached for a lantern hanging on the wall. She took it, pressed her fingers against the hot glass, and tossed it overhead at Goffee, who dodged away. The lantern smashed into the ground, and the blue light that leaked out faded back to orange and then died.

"Where do you get off," she demanded, "with your wits still about you under that wretched curse?!"

"Curse?" Goffee said. "Good lady, no, you misunderstand! We are not cursed. The Shades, they empowered us. To see through the dark as easily as good men can see through the light of day. But we are not good men, you see. After all, we are thieves, as you say."

"See, he agrees with me," Derek pointed out. "They all do. That means I was right."

Baxter took his cloak off the book and observed the effect. The blue fire was brighter, and Goffee appeared more animated. He stood up taller, arms wider, seemingly stronger just at a glance. The whole room turned to the same deep shade of blue as the book was fully exposed to the air.

"Give us the book," Goffee commanded. "It belongs to another."

"Perhaps," Baxter said, "but not you."

"Do you even know where to go with it?" Goffee asked.

Baxter didn't answer. He knew the answer was within, still hidden in the many exploits and adventures of its author, but he lacked the critical information at this most important moment. In his heart, he knew it was important to him. The task was an oath, sworn unto his late Master, and now that it was his, he could not revoke or renege it. But Goffee was right. He never considered truthfully whose hands the book was better off in.

"And thus did rise, like birds off the sands, a fire from this wanderer's hands."

A strange verse from a venerable voice filled the cave. The blue fires started to flicker chaotically and began shifting color. The thieves all looked for the source of the noise, but only Goffee seemed aware and turned to the cart of Yahid. The man stood with his hands up, cupping a surge of fire against his palm.

It burnt and wavered harmlessly, not even warming his hand, and grew higher.

"Ten hundred flames created ten hundred feathers and flew into the air beyond the reach of the core of the fire's breathing self. And so, it split, ten hundred pieces merging together, one hundred to each ten, until one hundred birds soared into creation from the fire made of the mage's hands!"

At his command, the fire exploded outward, and each great waft of flame turned into a flying, burning dove. They swarmed and filled the room with glaring light that blinded the blue eyes of every thief, including Goffee. To those unaffected, Baxter and his friends, they only saw the splendid glory of the dancing fire birds. One dove down and flew by Baxter's face, but he felt no flame and smelled no burning. The fire was alive and shaped and given some kind of congruous mind.

Like the magic he read in the tales of old. He smiled as he recognized the words at last. They were from a volume of Old World myths and legends, the tale of their great hero Runish who could speak to the spirits of fire and command them to dance at his command. Yahid stood with his arms out, waving the fire to fly further away while he whistled the call of a bird with pursed lips.

"Come on!" Yahid shouted. "Get on! We have to go!"

Baxter snapped out of his fascination and ran forward. Derek and Eidel ran after him. All three jumped onto the cart while Yahid went to the front. His faithful cart leaders, two rugged and lumpy-looking horses, started shuffling forward and pulled the cart up to speed while the dance of fire and lights flew on behind them. Goffee recovered as the presence of the book left, and the swarm of flaming birds lit fires on the exposed covering of the thieves, even on some of their faces.

One thief burned away entirely, first his dry clothing and then his physical form went gaseous and vanished. The light of the fire intensified and consumed them until their pitch-black skin poured out of the depleting, dried-out wrappings to reveal the death of a Shade beneath. Goffee was torn between watching the hissing shadow being destroyed and his escaping targets.

"Bugger," he muttered. He turned to the still-gathered thieves and pointed outward. "After them!" he commanded. "Down the same tunnel! Out the same pass! They can't get far even traveling all hours! Race them to Braat and hunt them down!"

The thieves under his command, men and Shades alike, regrouped and swarmed to the remaining carts even as their proper owners cowered away from them in fear. Goffee stepped out with his hands behind his back. One wrist shook in the gentle hold of his other hand. "This is one job I can't screw up," he said. "Just one job…." His nerves were growing more and more frazzled. It took minutes before the first rider went out through one of the many tunnels to pursue their targets.

The evening was still approaching, the light still ruled the outside, and those who dwelled in the dark were poorly equipped to deal with those who could choose to live in the light….

19

The cart sped over the sands. The rugged beasts who pulled the cart over the hard, rough terrain snorted and grumbled as they hauled the travelers through the beginning of the night. The sky was dark overhead, but there was light on the horizon. A beaming signal stood out from the surrounding terrain at the top of a hill untouched by either forest or grass. Just outside of Vincia, on the other side of the Starlook River, the lands changed drastically. The expansive pastures and prairies that made up the Empire ended where the foreign waters began.

There was still plant life, but it was short grass, squat shrubs, and trees that stood out from one another, rarely forming more than a copse of woods at a hilltop or in a ditch where the waters pooled. The rains were scarcer here than even mere miles away, and the water of the river did not spill out into the plains as the land sloped down northward to provide for the life of the Vincian lands in the foothills. The Old World settled a little higher, not high enough to be cold but high enough that the rain drained away from it.

Baxter remarked on the sight with reserved awe. They were still in a flight for their lives away from a band of terrible mercenaries under the will of the Shades, but the lights from Galiley were already fading and fusing with the sparkling lights of the stars. The only other source of light was ahead of them—at the end of their fast path through the distant hills.

"Sir Yahid," Baxter shouted from the back, "I regret to inform you all too late that we are being pursued by those who wish us harm, and I'm afraid we may lack the compensation to adequately make up for the extra effort you have undertaken to protect us."

"You are polite for a young man," Yahid replied. He spurred his desert beasts on, and they obligingly sped up. They were like horses but saggy and floppy, yet their strange forms did not lack in power. They looked, at a glance, briefly familiar as if Baxter had seen or read about them before.

"Could you tell me," Baxter asked, "where you're taking us?"

Yahid pointed ahead to the light. "A bastion," he said. "A bulwark against the stalkers of the night. The Gazing Tower."

"Hey," Derek called out, "just what was that back there? You had a bunch of birds that you lit on fire. Is that safe at all?"

"Those weren't birds," Baxter said. "One flew right next to my face. I saw it."

"Well, I saw plenty," Derek commented. "I saw us get led right into a trap by a man who admitted he was a thief, and then I saw you both try to talk me out of my suspicion like it was all fine and normal to be trusting him. Pardon me for saying it, but I think I've seen enough today."

"Rest, friends," Yahid said. "The Order is watching over you. The Abyss shall not swallow you up so easily."

"Who are you really?" Baxter asked.

Yahid turned with a smile, one that lifted his whole face up and turned him into a seemingly different man in an instant.

"I can tell you when it's safer," he said. The beasts of burden continued their trek. After an hour, during which the group all rested against the cradling backs of the barrels and caskets around them, the cart slowed, and the light became too harsh to bear even with closed eyes. Baxter had his hood to protect him, and he peered out from under the brim that hung over his forehead.

They were at the base of a mighty-looking tower. It was old but not decrepit, well-kept, and with recently masoned walls where the wind and elements had chipped some important parts away. The light from above was so great, it made the arid rocky floor seem like it was being beaten down by the midday sun. Baxter led the team out and guided them while they shielded their eyes fruitlessly from the light above them.

"Come in," Yahid offered. Baxter obliged while the other two followed his voice. At the base of the tower was a small incline that led to a heavy door.

Yahid stopped them there and put his hand up while he muttered something fast and unrecognizable. The door unlatched and opened—rather curiously, Baxter thought, since there was no knob, handle, or lock visible from the outside. It was just a heavy, flat plank of wood covering the internal mechanisms of some device he couldn't discern.

The inside of the tower was as impressive as the outside, but for different reasons. It was wider than it appeared, with desks built into walls and bookshelves that scaled only to shoulder height, dividing the room into quarters. At the opposite side were two matching stairways that spiraled up along the outer edge of the inner wall. It reminded Baxter of the Archive he had left behind. The workstations looked similar to his as did the stacks upon stacks of books from all eras and all places.

"Another library?" Derek asked.

"Very nearly," Yahid said. "Please, come upstairs. We shall explain things there."

"If it's all the same," Derek said as he found a place to rest the book once more, "I'd like to keep both my hands free for any further talking up any stairs to any place I haven't been before."

"That is fair," Yahid allowed. "I will introduce myself first, then, friends. I am Yahid Yahazour, Sixth Heir of the House of Many Forests, in the place you call the Old World. I am also a member of a certain group that has sought to protect you and empower you, a group that Master Lothan had also joined."

"Master?" Baxter said quietly. "You…you knew of him?"

"I have met him many times," Yahid said. "It pained me to hear of this attack, but such assaults are not unfamiliar to us. For a very long time, we have prepared for this day, though we knew not when or how it would happen until the book resurfaced, and its power was reignited."

Baxter looked over at the book on the table. The *Daemondimonium* held its place, separate from the sandstone counter hewn from the same material as the walls of the great tower, seeming a dark, rectangular blot like the shadow of a passing cloud over a great sea of off-white sand. Baxter was shaken by a hand on his shoulder, which he instinctively shook off. It was Yahid's hand, and Baxter backed away from him in shame.

"The book is very powerful," Yahid informed him. "And very important."

"We can tell," Eidel said, snippy as usual, even against a figure of some authority. She had reached her breaking point. Between being shown up, having her father's curse outright dismissed by the only person among them who could read about it, and on the travel out of her homeland—the Empire that had entirely made up her world until this point—she was long overdue to snap. "Important to a group of demonic monsters from the slithering gates of a shadowy hell. And all its purpose was entrusted to this one. Of all people, a habitual reader with no more sense for the world or proper politics among the Guilds than this one over here." She pointed angrily to Derek, who seemed confused and looked behind him to the upper wall.

"Yes," Yahid said with a sigh. "It was worrisome to learn the dreams that told of this event came from one so young as you, Mr. Baxter."

"My dreams?" he asked. He made a whisper of revelation. "The Abyss."

"Indeed," Yahid said. "There is much to explain, but first—"

"But first," a lady interrupted from on high as she descended to the ground floor. The woman was dressed for travel in robes similar to Yahid's, long and light and airy-looking with a mantle of cloth wrapped around her neck and a veil of silk cast over her hair. She was about as elderly as Yahid but hid all signs or traces with perfectly applied glamour. "Further introductions are in order for this Revision to the Lore."

"Sir Yahid," Baxter whispered, "is she supposed to be here?"

"Oh, how charming," the woman said. "You have your Master's sense of humor. I thought you'd be glad to know that he's alive, but you already seem so keen to replace him that perhaps I should withhold the proof."

"Master is alive?!" Baxter exclaimed.

"Well, I feel like a jerk now," Derek said. "He's a tough old geezer."

"Gazer," Yahid corrected. "We are the Gazers, ones who watch over the Abyss, where the histories of the world encircle toward a shared—"

"No, he was right," the lady informed Yahid. "He was making a joke."

"Was I?" Derek asked curiously.

Baxter broke the flow of the exchange by dragging the book toward the place where a chair was pushed under the overhang of the desk. He pulled it open and let the pages fall in thuds into each other to reveal the opening illustration.

"Please, tell me," Baxter began, "if Master is alive, did he impart any further instructions on what we must do with this book?"

"Well," she said, "you are quick to the point. Dutiful adherence is a quality sorely lacking from Lothan's repertoire. But how charmless of me to denigrate my colleague in front of one who cares about him so deeply. I am Madam Suttwood of the Guild Conglomerate."

Eidel gasped. For her and the Porters, the name of Suttwood was as ubiquitous as the names of the ruling royalty were for the common peasantry of Checcheri. She was like a celebrity and a powerful authority figure combined.

"Hi," Derek said.

Eidel nudged him in the leg to move aside so she could take his spot and get closer.

"I'm Master Lothan's apprentice, Baxter," he said. "I…I regret to admit that I still don't quite know what I'm doing, and now I am possessed by far more curiosity than fear at the possibility of preceding further. I must know, what exactly has all this been for?"

"He thought you might have trouble learning," she said, "what with all the running for your life to be done. It was fortunate Yahid and I were on our way through to this tower so we could take you in as a temporary measure."

"From the Shades," Baxter realized in a dark tone. His knowledge of them from beginning to end was spotty. Those he knew in life were ruthless hunters, but the ones in the book were passive and docile. Yet, he'd only just begun the great compendium of Plattius's knowledge. What remained to learn he could only imagine. It was only after seeing the danger that he understood the importance of what he had to learn.

"This tower," she explained, "was created to stand against the Shades long ago. During the Age of Conquest, when lords raised armies to siege the lands of others in uneven, imbalanced, and constant conflict, which lasted generations, one lord from the southern lands of the Old World, from the once prosperous kingdom of Shish, brought forth a terror in the night. He made a contract with the Shades and wielded them as a terrible weapon, and his force became unstoppable, all but for the lords in the northern lands and the khans to the far east. Together, those forces combined and drove them back, wielding the light that chased their shadowy forms away, and they did all of that using the knowledge compiled in that book."

She pointed to it, and the grimoire splayed open to the caricature of the author and the many languages his name was written in. They were a wreath of camaraderie, even tongues of the Old World, of the cities that were razed in the wake of the Shades. All those he met in his travels, all those he spread his words to carried his legacy on to build towers and share that knowledge with others. Baxter finally felt he understood the true intention of the book. Its beginning was changed from its ending, not in the text, but in the intent. It was a passing journal of a man seeking fortune and the strange things he saw along the way, but what it inspired thereafter caused the world to change.

"So, someone made a new contract," Derek summed up. His astuteness captured everyone's attention in the room. "And that contract is to get the book…for some reason."

"To stop it from propagating, maybe," Baxter said. "Something this significant couldn't be kept in the Archive for no reason. It's more than just a book or a curio for some nobleman to gawk at. This is…as you said, Sir Yahid, it is important."

"Very," Yahid confirmed. "Though, we do not know the reason they have come to claim it, they have, and that must be abetted. This tower was made using the magic of recreation. The light above will shine for six days and six nights, and on the seventh it shall ascend high into the sky for six hundred days and nights as a star shimmering above before it can be called down again."

"How high up even is that?" Derek asked as he marveled at the ceiling toward the light high above.

"It will be a high order," Madam Suttwood said, "but you will have to rise to your station in the short time of a week."

"My station?" Baxter asked. She turned to the other two, to Eidel who stood in confused reverence, and Derek, the tallest and burliest in the whole room, chest out and arms crossed, his rugged jaw jutting out in a commanding scowl. Titles meant nothing before his brawn and confidence. Madam Suttwood observed him very carefully, to the discomfort of Yahid.

"Yes," Yahid said, veering the discussion back on course. "Your higher purpose. Your goal. What you were sent out to do."

"Which is hidden in the text and context of the book," Baxter continued. "And, possibly, the meta-text."

"The Living Lore," Madam Suttwood said. The words tugged at Baxter's ear. "That is what you were being trained for all along, apprentice scholar. Not only to learn the *how* and *when*, or the *whom* or the *where*, but the *why* and *when again*, and the *where else*, and the *what now*. You are invited to the heritage of mystics through time to invoke the practiced magics inherited to the world through the heroes and legends of the past so you may reforge the path that saved the world long before."

As Madam Suttwood spoke, a brief wind rustled from within the tower, seemingly from all around her, and fluttered her skirts up inches off the ground. Once she finished, it fell, and many pages were scattered from their flimsy bindings. She clicked her tongue at the brief mess as she looked around.

"Those fire birds…?" Baxter asked.

"Indeed," Yahid said. "That is the power you must learn to wield. To recite the texts of events that once occurred. In doing so, you reread the passage of history to recur, to incite events of the world's mythical history, the Living Lore, to resurface. And as the words are spoken, and the Great Eye sees your words spoken into the fabric of the Present, it shall overwrite the utterance with imagery of the Past, merging the text together. To Transcribe the ancient past onto the present. That is the source of my power and the power of the Gazers."

"He has to be old to do that?" Derek asked. Eidel jabbed him in the ribs and he gasped out a snort, trying to stifle his laughter.

"The Gazers are watchers of the Abyss," Madam Suttwood said in a serious tone. "We are keepers of the hidden truth, of the knowledge of the ocean of death beneath the surface of our world, and those who are born without light and life yet act as if they live regardless on the border of both worlds. Those are the Shades. Though, you may know far more by what is contained within the book."

"You haven't read it?" Baxter asked.

"I haven't the time," she said quite casually. "Our purpose is to guide society away from studies outside their own nature, and more importantly, to manage the revision of the Living Lore. The lands of Vincia are unique to history. They are the first of their kind in all writings. To properly uphold them, certain members of the private parties must delegate the passing of powers to the ruling classes. To prevent another Age of Conquest from repeating."

"There is a great deal to learn," Yahid said. "About the Revisions of history, the cycles of repeating text, the nature of the Living Lore. Though we have spent much of our lives learning and understanding these things and making great use of them for the benefit of others, it falls on you now to seal the Abyss away once again. You must become the Loremaster, find the path walked once before, and act upon it for the benefit once gained and recorded in the living history of the world.

"And you two," Yahid continued, looking at Derek and Eidel, "have gone through a great deal of strife to assist the apprentice until he could reach us in this sanctuary. His journey will be difficult alone, but together, as three, you can protect—"

"You're not getting rid of me," Derek said, interrupting the discussion as he assumed it led to his dismissal. He stepped up next to Baxter and held him in place with his stiff hand pressed against the boy's back. The pat he gave was so forceful it flipped Baxter's hood up. "At least, not until you can carry that book on your own."

Baxter undid his hood and looked up with a smile. "That sounds fair. The day I can carry it in my arms without stopping or letting go from dawn to dusk, you'll be exonerated from my service."

"Okay, well," Derek said, "let's have it to a great exoneration together!" Baxter grinned at his friend's enthusiasm and let his misuse of language slide right off his shoulders.

"And you?" Madam Suttwood asked Eidel. "You've ported them expertly across the wilderness.

With this journey now done, and a new one beginning, is there some other place you'd rather be?"

Eidel looked at Baxter and then the book. He caught her gaze, and they exchanged a serious expression. As presumptuous as he was, in her opinion, he was also smart. He knew what she wanted and showed her the resolve needed to accomplish her own mission.

"My father," she answered, "is cursed like those in the cavern of the city. I agreed to accompany them in exchange that he finds a cure for that curse and a way to remove it. My job is not over until that payment has been rendered. And I, as a Porter, take pride in what I am, though my house is small, I will see that task through."

Madam Suttwood smiled and gave Eidel a gentle pat on the head, which the girl privately savored with a thin-lipped grin. "The road ahead six days from now," she told them, "will be a dangerous one. Even just beginning to read through the Walker's book, you should know that there are dangers beyond what beasts and myths you already know."

"Yes," Baxter agreed, "but how many remain? Has time not taken its toll on that land and its vast nothingness to deplete it of these monstrosities?"

"Like all things in history," Yahid said, "its problems also recur. Monsters do not die. Though their forms may change, obstacles will remain the same across this path. You must learn it, memorize it, and when the time arrives, you shall recite from it what must occur to overcome the hurdles history places in your way. You do not walk the path of your own story. Regardless, it is a path that will save the world from a dark incursion."

"Okay," Baxter said. He took a deep breath in and rubbed his eyes. "That's pressure."

"Come on, man," Derek said. He pulled out the chair and pushed Baxter down onto it. "Saving the world, mate! And all you have to do is read!"

"That's not exactly—" Yahid started but was interrupted when Baxter clapped his hands together and sat up straight. He looked around for a lantern or candle and found a shutter instead. When he opened it, the bright light from high above was filtered in through a network of mirrors, crystals, and reflective tubes over the swath of his desk. The *Daemondimonium*, and the archaic depiction of its author, stared back up at him from the light, still darkened by its very weight like a shadow sticking out from the bright ground below.

"I suppose I should start, then," Baxter said. In those few words, many things began. He spoke with the same density at the text before him, layered with many meanings and secrets yet to be found.

Thus, the cycle of Lore began anew, and a new Master began his work of reading….

20

Morning came to Galiley. The brigands assembled through the caves and back into the subterranean cavern with their heads low. Some did not make it back as the morning sun dissolved them, leaving only their confused horses to wander with a heap of empty, armored clothing dangling off their saddles.

Those who returned were greeted to nothing but shadows ahead. Even as the torches in their hands burned away, they saw nothing beyond their own bodies. It was not the shadows of the underground where the sun couldn't reach that blinded them but something more physically present. A thick and permeable darkness like a cloud of ink surrounded them, then all at once, grappled them with appendages like many hands running over their bodies.

After a blind, deaf travel through the dark, the marked thieves were deposited into the carriage dock and bathed in sinister blue lights. Those who rejected their position out of fear and confusion or showed regret or tried to turn away from their duties were turned back by the light in their eyes. Their bodies quit on them, and they shambled with limp arms and craned necks.

Those more willing and more reverent than fearful took to their knees and held their hands in position, in the shape of a mountain with peaks of fingertips tilted upside down. Goffee was at the lead of that group, those who retained their minds under the duress of the vast powers before them. The Shades in the cavern were not common ones lent to their cause or tracking the bookkeepers. The first to appear was wrapped in fine cloths and silks imitating the dressings of the Old World cultures from head to foot. It spoke in a whisper, as though it drew in breath to form its words.

"Lord Victus approaches," the herald spoke. "He who has bound many has come to speak to his first adherent of the High World lands."

Goffee tilted his head up. From the rear of the cave, the shadows flooded in like a surge of river waters were filling the passages of the long-dammed cave. When the tide of shadows receded, a shimmer of metallic armor penetrated the dark, and the vision of Victus stood before Goffee with a heavy metal instrument in his hand, a solid rod with no edge or piercing point, tip-down to the floor. He rested his armored palm upon it like a scepter and waved his free hand for his thief to rise.

"They escaped," Victus hissed.

Goffee stood and avoided the eyes of his apparent lord. "That they did," he said. "But-but we know where they are! A place your kind can't go, yes, but that is not to say it is a place impenetrable. We are thieves. We-we are experts of stealth and sneaking. Give us a few days, or perhaps a week at the most, and I promise you we can infiltrate their walls against their light and retrieve the book. Just one chance against the luck of the world! This time, there won't be interruption. This time—"

Victus grabbed Goffee's face and growled. Goffee struggled briefly before his body was emaciated. The heft of his figure shriveled inward, and his face went shallow. His life drained away, and he was left half-living, eyes glowing blue, voice lost to a hollow, whispering groan as he shuffled his way to the side where the other mindless revelers went.

Victus looked in his hand where the steam-like wisp of life sucked into his palm. He hissed as it entered him and stoked the fire in his eyes brighter. "It has been written," Victus said. All lifted their hands to his words. Their fingers pointed up, a mountain rising from the dark. "It shall be done." The cavern filled with darkness again, and the Man from the Abyss laid in wait once more. To try again for his chance to change the history before him and darken the pages of the Living Lore.

New Book Releases

Thank you for reading *The Shades of the Abyss*! This is the first book in *The Living Lore* series. Sign up for our newsletter for updates on new releases at: twistedkeypublishing.com

You may also follow the authors on Amazon and Goodreads for updates on works-in-progress and Goodreads giveaways.

For short stories, sneak peaks and early access to our ready-to-publish books, follow and support us at Patreon: patreon.com/twistedkeypublishing

SHORT STORIES

PANTECH CHRONICLES
SHADOWFALCON
BOOK I
F. LOCKHAVEN
M.A. OWENS

F. Lockhaven is one of Grace Lockhaven's author pen names, primarily focused on Teen and Young Adult Science Fiction and Fantasy.

If you love reading Premature Teen Fantasy stories, you may enjoy reading the following series:

QUEST CHASERS

Book 1: The Deadly Cavern
Book 2: The Screaming Mummy

Book 1

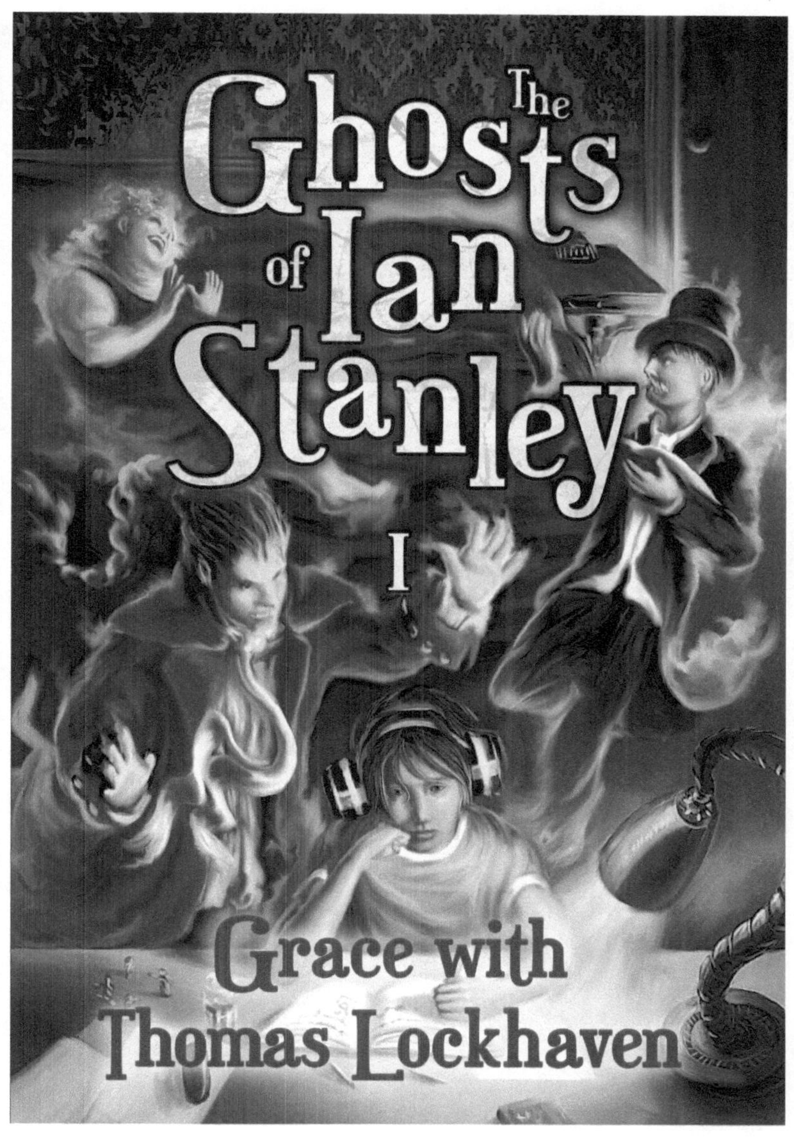